LAREDO ROAD

LAREDO ROAD

Will C. Brown

Thorndike Press • Chivers Press
Thorndike, Maine USA   Bath, England

This Large Print edition is published by Thorndike Press, USA and by Chivers Press, England.

Published in 2000 in the U.S. by arrangement with Golden West Literary Agency.

Published in 2000 in the U.K. by arrangement with Golden West Literary Agency.

U.S. Hardcover 0-7862-2277-8 (Western Series Edition)
U.K. Hardcover 0-7540-4029-1 (Chivers Large Print)
U.K. Softcover 0-7540-4030-5 (Camden Large Print)

The text of this Large Print edition is unabridged. Other aspects of the book may vary from the original edition.

Set in 16 pt. Plantin by Juanita Macdonald.

Printed in the United States on permanent paper.

British Library Cataloguing-in-Publication Data available

Library of Congress Cataloging-in-Publication Data

Brown, Will C., 1905–
    Laredo Road / Will C. Brown.
        p. cm.
    ISBN 0-7862-2277-8 (lg. print : hc : alk. paper)
    1. Large type books. I. Title.
PS3552.R739 L37   2000
813′.54—dc21   99-048648

1/28/00 GALE 21.95

LAREDO ROAD

1

Cibolo Creek was on a rampage.

The caretaker at the stage station watched with superstitious disfavor as the freak torrent poured down from the Texas Big Bend. He saw Laredo Road all at once come to a dead watery stop at the crossing where yesterday there had been nothing but a damp trickle through the rocky bottom of the arroyo fording place.

Hagerman knew that the flood would wear itself out by the ferocity of its quick spree and that the crossing would soon fall back to a trickle. But until the spree was over, there was no place to ford the creek for miles east or west. The unexpected arrival of the strangers, a gaunt homesteader and his wife, who were the first travelers to be held up by the flooded creek, increased Hagerman's strange uneasiness.

The caretaker kept his own cranky aloofness when the transient couple pitched their camp at a distance from his station building to wait out the high water. Hagerman thought the man appeared to be nursing some strong, hidden agitation, the way he formed brusque questions about other fordings places and whether other travelers had arrived from the north. Once, the woman got as far as asking Hagerman something about "the El Bar place," but her husband shut her up with a quick look.

Hagerman could not tell whether the stranger was satisfied or disappointed that there was nobody else at the crossing. The rest of the day he kept wondering. In his lonely existence, small things loomed large to Hagerman.

The caretaker was a big-boned, stolid workman, absent-eyed and untidy, who did the simple chores and had forgotten there was a world out beyond where once he had squared young shoulders and known ambition. Long ago, he had seen his bride die from an Indian arrow shot through her breast, and that had ended his challenge to the frontier. He lived out his time now on the pittance paid him by the Southwest Texas Stage Company to look after the station and horse pen. He disliked the alien noise of the flooded Cibolo because at night time it sounded to his memory something like Indians coming.

Not many people traveled Laredo Road. Its faint tracks started at Laredo and extended northwest, up across the prickly pear, chaparral, mesquite and crazy canyons, eventually crossed Devil's River, to Sonora, and on to Angelo. The stage company was on its way to going broke and owed Hagerman three months' pay.

When the middle-aged nester pair had first driven up, the man had examined the flooded fording place as if it were an animal never seen before. The couple had held an undertoned caucus while they watched the torrent from the wagon seat.

Later, Hagerman seemed to remember that they led a saddle horse behind their prairie wagon. The man told Hagerman his name was Barton. He was a knife-eyed, underfed slat of a man with gray stickery whiskers, and he and the woman were southbound on the Road from somewhere that Hagerman never correctly heard.

The couple picked a place in some stunted mesquites and low cedars beyond the corner of the 'dobe, and Barton set up a typical nester's camp by tossing out a few articles from the wagon. By nightfall they had a fire going and an iron frijole pot simmering.

The woman, small in stature though full-bosomed, with her wind-tanned features composed but mostly hidden by the drape of a big starchless sunbonnet, mixed *penole* cornbread. The two of them sat together for a time on the wagon seat that Barton had removed from the wagon and watched the road far off where it vanished in the northward haze.

When they spoke, their words seemed cautious, and briefly murmured. Once, the woman peered north up the Road and said, "I wonder if he'll come?" The man shook his head quickly at her and stalked off to look at the flooded crossing again.

The Texas panic of 1873–1874 had carried its momentum into this following year. Poverty and failure were everywhere; and to see whipped-out, land-beat homesteaders trying to get from where they'd been to somewhere else, was nothing new to Hagerman.

He blankly noticed that the Bartons piddled about their poor-man's camp in the weedy flat the next morning. The man acted aimless at times, going off somewhere in the creek willows, then coming back and sitting beside the woman for a while on the wagon seat and poking at the fire.

The weather turned warm toward noon of the second day, hinting of the hellishly hot border summer on its way. The Bartons' bean pot simmered again. Barton cleaned a shotgun. Hagerman fed the horses in the pen, then napped in the shade of a cedar stand back of the corral.

Northward, three men rode single file on Laredo Road. The riders were southbound, headed toward the Cibolo stage station and the fording.

The man in the lead was colored to a tobacco brown by the border sun. His close-set eyes worked in perpetual calculation. His body was heavy, his face was thick ridged, and his muscles strained the stitching of his clothes.

The second man rode awkwardly. His thin, limp-hung frame swayed with the horse's plod in the lanky hungry build of youth, and his brown-checked, red-fuzzed, high-boned face hung down so his sombrero would shade the high sun.

He rode with both thin hands on his saddle horn. When he pulled at his hat brim, or brushed a fly away from the sweat of his nose, he raised both hands caught together in brass cuffs with three small chain links between his wrists.

The rider just behind, bringing up the rear of the single file procession, showed a washed-out countenance and a chinless head that bobbled high on his thin red neck. Like the dark brawny man in the lead, this one also sported a silver-plated shield on his jacket front. Their badges played off sun rays, as though signaling to the country that there came the Law. The manacled young man on the middle horse twisted back and spoke to the rear guard rider, saying that he sure could use a drink of water. The answer was an obscene short word. The rider in front impatiently flung his arm in a motion for the others to close ranks.

They rode tiredly, men and horses. It had been a long trip up for the two lawmen, a long ride back from Angelo for all three. Now the Cibolo was in sight. Beyond that, no more than four hours, would be trail's end. Laredo.

Navarro, the deputy in the lead, thought of the one-thousand-dollar reward he would get for the return of the young man known to him as Rusty Ferris.

Rusty Ferris, in the middle, did not think about much of anything; but the blurred hell of the mess he was in, and what a firing squad would be like in Mexico. They would give him no chance, no fair trial. Even Navarro's extradition order had been faked.

Deputy Lenman, in the rear, worried that

he might have trouble with Navarro over his cut of the thousand dollars. After all, he knew Navarro well.

Dewey Lane came upon the Road from a quartering angle, striking the wheel trace from straight north soon after sighting the Cibolo tree line.

He rode from last night's lost campsite, coming on like a shadow off the lonesome country and pleased to see the straggly course of the creek show itself. With journey's end now so near, the Panhandle sun wrinkles webbing his eyes began to mesh with quickening interest for what he saw. The sun wrinkles made false age tracks in his lean features. Another noticeable age contrast was in the hard, stained look of his leg revolver and faded holster, and the obviously store-new sheen of the Winchester carbine and its bright leather boot. In addition to the tall man, who was no lightweight, his big black horse also was burdened with bulging saddlebags and a thick blanket roll, suggesting a man headed somewhere with the intention to stay a while. Or going a long way.

The black horse gave the air a muzzle poking and, smelling water, stretched its sore stride. Dewey shed his own tiredness to stirrup up tall and study a thin blue smear barely showing in the southward haze. Hills of Old Mexico. His dried lips pulled down in a thin grin.

There was a Latin phrase for his journey at this stage. If he could remember it. Something like *in utrumque paratus . . .* ready for either, he thought it meant — he could stay or keep going. He spat dry dust toward the black's left ear. Memory spat back. Half a dozen Latin phrases, maybe, and a college boxing championship. Meager chips, he admitted, to pick up from that year they'd sent him East to school. Eon before last, that was, with long trail drives, saloon fights and the weekly newspaper blanking out the time since. His father had left him the struggling newspaper, and that was about all; and he had been six months in Montana before he knew of either the death or inheritance. The type case turned out to be no place for a man with far horizons built into his sinews, so he had got rid of the miserable layout at the first opportunity.

Now he reflected that when he had traded McCall the starved-out print shop at Caprock a month back, for the deed to El Bar Ranch in this far-off border land, the old man had glibly assured him that this was God's country down here with the friendliest people on earth.

What people?

He had seen no two-legged creature since a Mexican wood hauler on the Lampasas, four days back. The rattlers, the scrawny coyotes and sand crawlers had seemed to him a particularly unfriendly breed. God's country. That must have been the rye talking in McCall. Well, now, Dewey Lane owned a dirty handful of it somewhere around here. If he could find the handful.

The new owner of El Bar Ranch on the Cibolo flung sweat off his jaw and strained his hearing to identify a mysterious sound. Unexplainable, but it was running water, a torrent, sounded like, and not a cloud anywhere bigger than the black's bit foam.

Just before noon, he pulled the sweaty black at right angles off the Laredo Road, to the yard of the 'dobe stage house. At the same time, he sighted a dust trace of oncoming riders far north behind him. He saw with surprise the flooded arroyo, something he had never expected in the dry border country. He took in with a quick look the crumbling mud walls of the stage station, the horse pen at the back, the nester outfit camped in the mesquites below.

Nobody was in sight at the corral; so he

unsaddled, cared for his horse, turned it loose in the pen and drank from the windmill pipe at the water trough. He had a moment of indecision about his new Winchester carbine.

He was reluctant to leave it in its saddle boot, with the saddle spread on the top fence rail. Yet he disliked walking to the building with the rifle under his arm. He wore the holstered .44 Colt, and to stalk up there with the carbine beside would look like he packed an unseemly amount of armament. His final decision, though, was to carry the Winhester rather than leave it. Somehow this place looked anything but friendly.

Hagerman came from somewhere, and their courses merged at the back corner. They inventoried one another in a moment of double scrutiny, then Dewey briefly introduced himself. Things still seemed mighty unfriendly.

The stage, southbound from Angelo and Sonora, careened southward but still far up-country from the Cibolo crossing. The crippled man, Benecke, was on the seat fighting the four wiry mules. He rode the waving top deck in an odd contortion of shape, same as when afoot — his affliction being such that when he faced one direction the old broken hip and crookedly healed leg seemed to want to go the opposite way. He looked miserable, but actually was as comfortable there as anywhere else. The two passengers were the uncomfortable ones.

When Benecke had made the Sonora stop, the hostler had jerked a thumb toward the two waiting passengers and grunted, "Show girls," from the corner of his mouth.

From the time the stage took off, there was little opportunity for conversation, and the two seemed absorbed in their own thoughts. When they had anything to say to one another their words were brief and low. The pretty pink one, older than the other, smiled artificially when Benecke leaned over to look down at them. The younger was plainer because of a freckled nose, though not unattractive. Benecke finally got the idea that the older one was engaged in an inner skirmish with some problem, and that the younger rode as a sort of self-appointed lookout for the other. Once he saw the older touch her finger to an eyelash and he detected the tear.

The stage racket softened just then in a momentary stretch of sand, and in the unexpected quiet the driver caught fragments of murmured words.

"I keep wondering if he will come this way . . ."

"He will, Cherry!"

"Oh, I pray we will find him!"

"Don't give up, ever!"

The wheels thundered on rocky ground again. Benecke yelled at his mules and cracked his whip. The dust swirled up as the day warmed, and Laredo Road came inside and fogged the air, coating the girls with its white powder.

It seemed an eternity until the brakes squealed, the hurricane beneath their bodies calmed, and the spokes rattled to a slower turn. The two craned their necks for a look. Some words of Benecke's drifted down, broken apart in the sentence, but inside the stage they heard "crossing" and "goddam *flood!*" "The Gibbons Sisters," Cherry and May, frowned a moment before setting their features pleasantly.

2

Hagerman opened the plank door to one of the two small rooms off the east end of the long main room, and a black tarantula hurried under the dusty iron cot in the corner.

"It's fifty cents for all night."

"No bargain, is it?" Dewey smiled.

He brought his gear to the tiny bedroom and walked back to the kitchen.

"Do you think I might get across tomorrow?"

"Might. Might not." Hagerman reached over to whack a baby centipede on the counter with a butcher knife. "It ought to run down by tomorrow. Now I got to get ready for the stage, when it comes."

"I'm looking for the El Bar Ranch," Dewey said conversationally.

Hagerman carefully replaced the lid on the chili pot. He mumbled, "El Bar." Then, "Man named McCall tried it once. Homesteader outfit."

"McCall. That's right. I own it now."

Hagerman worried a stick of mesquite into the firebox. "You ain't got much. Trouble, mostly."

"How's that?"

"You know about the Tembler crowd? The cattle outfit east of El Bar?"

"Haven't had the pleasure."

Hagerman said shortly, "Mean hunch of bastards." and turned to his cooking counter. "I got to get dinner."

Dewey ignored his dismissal. "I don't remember that McCall mentioned his neighbors."

"Not apt to mention the Temblers, if he was selling you his place."

"I traded him a weekly newspaper for it, and we both warned the other that he was getting cheated. What's bothering the Temblers?"

Hagerman fixed a crafty stare on Dewey for a moment, then blanked his features again. "I reckon McCall didn't mention the Sorro outfit in Mexico, either. Or the law in Laredo. "

"Do you mean Sorro the bandit? I've heard of him. But not the Laredo law and not the Temblers. What's that got to do with El Bar?"

"You aim to try to run the claim?"

"Is it worth the effort?"

20

"Naw. Not from the way I've heard it. You'd be just as well off to forget it and keep ridin'."

"What I almost had in mind," Dewey admitted, as much to himself as to the man working at the cook table. He turned away, seeing that Hagerman was finished with talking. He walked into the yard and studied the dust trace northward again. Not the stage. Horsemen. The riders would be here in half an hour. He moved on across the clearing. The sounds of the running arroyo came to his ears like bursts of happy music. He had not heard so much water pouring in all his years in the parched plains country.

A sunbonneted figure in calico had come up a little way from the wagon in the sapling mesquites. Standing at the edge of the station clearing, Dewey saw the woman as she stooped to snap with care the thin stems of a scrawny bunch of bluebonnets.

She straightened and their eyes met.

Dewey saw the worn, patient mouth lines, and the half-frightened shadow that passed over her face and gave way to birdlike caution. Dewey nodded and touched his hat brim. She moved her lips for just the faintest responding smile, then turned back to her wagon.

Dewey watched her purposeful walk until

she was almost to her cook fire. Then he pulled himself out of a momentary twinge of loneliness and walked downgrade to the rocky ledge to look at the rampaging Cibolo.

When instinct told him somebody was watching from behind, he threw a quick backward glance. He saw a gaunt man in gallused union suit standing on the slope above, peering down at him. Dewey waited, then made a motion of greeting. The man jerked a tentative acknowledgment, hooked his thumbs in his pants, and trudged back toward the wagon. It was plain that the woman had told the man, and the man had come to look him over.

Dewey strained to see southeastward across the flooded draw, into the sun haze and brushy mounds stretching off to the bottom edge of an empty sky. He wondered if he was seeing the El Bar claim somewhere out there.

He admitted to himself that the whole vague idea of settling down on a border claim he had never laid eyes on was a fool-hardy one from the beginning. Was he to be a lifetime drifter? The sketchy information that Hagerman had given him kept coming back to whet his interest in El Bar in a way he had not known before. Why so much opposition from the Temblers? It was evident that they had run off McCall, and that they would like to pick up the El Bar title when the claim was revoked for nonoccupancy. A thing like that sharpened some of the fullness off a man's long lonesome ride. Why had nobody ever stayed on the El Bar claim?

Whistling tunelessly he walked back to the building. The riders, three in number, were now materializing in a dusty procession. Hagerman ambled out to stand near Dewey and look. Mr. and Mrs. Barton arose from their wagon seat and they, too, faced anxiously north toward the Road.

3

Navarro came forward first. The other deputy stayed on his horse. Rusty Ferris, in handcuffs, stayed put, too, waiting for instructions.

The lawman made a half salute toward Hagerman, then studied Dewey. He turned around and sharply called, "Lenman!"

Lenman pulled his carbine from its saddle boot and held it in one hand.

Navarro spoke. "Who you got here, Hagerman?"

"Just him." Hagerman thumbed toward Dewey Lane. "Who's that you got?"

"Name's Rusty Ferris," replied Navarro. "Killed a man in Mexico."

Rusty blurted, "in self-defense!" Navarro scowled.

Dewey watched with curious interest both the officers and their prisoner. Rusty didn't look like an outlaw. Of the two, he thought, the lawman Navarro looked like the meanest customer.

Navarro moved heavily about. "What's the wagon down there, Hagerman?"

"Homesteader and his wife."

"How long's the creek been up?"

"Day before yesterday."

"No way to cross?"

"Nope."

Navarro swore. "Means we'll have to spend the night. You got a room we can lock him in?"

"I reckon so."

Navarro stalked past Hagerman. "I didn't get your name, mister."

"Dewey Lane. Yours?"

"Navarro. Deputy sheriff. What's your business here, Lane?"

"I'm headed south, going to look at some land."

Navarro asked sharply, "He all right, Hagerman?"

Hagerman looked blankly at Dewey as if trying to remember his credentials. "Yeah. He's all right, Navarro."

Navarro explained. "We've got a bad one here. Being extradited to Mexico. In a situation like this, I take no chances. I don't aim to lose him."

"Smart thing," Dewey murmured.

"Yeah. You never know when a prisoner might have friends. A gang, maybe, that

would like to jump me and turn him loose."
He extended his left hand. "I'll take that
gun, if you don't mind."

"I mind."

Navarro's mouth hardened. "It's just a
precaution. We don't know you. I don't
want a lot of guns around for him to grab at.
We got this man to hold overnight. Everybody will get their weapons back when we
leave."

Dewey reached for his gun and Navarro
moved quickly. "Hold it! I'll take it out!"

Navarro slipped the Colt free and stepped
back. Dewey watched the tired prisoner,
who had dismounted and now stood a pace
ahead of Lenman who held the carbine.

In that moment, while the whole party
seemed buckled in its tracks, Rusty raised
his head and food off toward the wagon
camp. Almost immediately, he lowered his
eyes again to his handcuffed wrists.

Navarro pointed toward the wagon.
"What they got in guns down there?"

"I seen a shotgun," Hagerman told him.

"Go get it. Explain to the man. Bring him
on in the house, Lenman."

Lenman moved the carbine. "Go on in
there, Rusty."

Navarro said to Dewey, "You move on in
front of me."

Dewey went ahead. Navarro made a quick search of the long dim room. "Whose stuff in the little room?"

Dewey said, "Mine. I'm bunking in there."

"Not now you ain't. Any guns?"

"Winchester carbine. The rest is saddlebags, canteen and blanket roll."

"You move 'em out here."

Dewey went in and packed out his gear. Navarro took the carbine out of his arms. "Hagerman can bed you in the main room here with us. I want that other little room for Rusty, seeing it's got a lock and key, and I'd rather the one next to it stay empty."

Dewey dumped his gear in a corner, thinking there was nothing wrong with a lawman being like this. Rusty Ferris had come inside the door by now, trailed by Lenman. The prisoner narrowed his gaze around at the shadows.

"That room," Navarro motioned. "It's got a lock outside. Check the window in there, Lenman."

Rusty sniffed. "Chili! We going to eat now?"

"After a while."

"How about a drink of water?"

"I don't hear very good, kid."

Dewey planted his shoulder against the

27

wall and continued to watch Rusty. "What did he do?" he asked quietly of Navarro.

"Murder. Below the border." Navarro was busy beating the dust off his clothes. "We brought him back from Angelo. For extradition."

Rusty laughed, one short scornful sound. "Extradition, hell!"

Navarro made a quick step. His big hand flashed. Rusty jerked but the blow grazed his ear.

Dewey heard Rusty laugh again defiantly. This time Navarro was quicker. The back of his hand smashed Rusty in the mouth. The manacled wrists flew up for a shield and blood ran on his lips.

Lenman came out. "It's all right. The window in there won't raise no more than six inches. Room's as tight as a jail cell."

Rusty said, "I tell you I'm dying for a drink of water."

"Get the hell in, that room!"

The small room, with a lock on the door and a key outside in the lock, yawned in semi-gloom at the far corner of the main room. Next to it, in the right corner, was the open door to the room Dewey had just vacated. Rusty started slowly for the room with the lock. Through the door opening, Dewey could see the shadows, the iron cot in the corner, the window beyond with the small air opening.

Rusty suddenly whirled completely about, half raising his manacled hands. He looked directly at Dewey. "I'm being railroaded, mister! They're going to have me shot because —"

Navarro smashed a spread palm against the scrawny chest, and the prisoner careened into his cell. Navarro gritted, "You want to keep yappin' or you want some water?"

"Water," the youth groaned.

Navarro shoved Rusty's legs with his boot toe to make way for the door to close. Rusty struggled up. "Damn you, don't stomp me, Navarro."

Lenman slammed the door and turned the key. Navarro took the key from him and carefully worked it into his pants pocket, smiling. He spoke to Dewey. "That boy's an awful liar."

Hagerman brought in Barton's shotgun.

"Put all the guns in the closet yonder and lock it," Navarro said to Lenman. "Hagerman's rifle included. I'm going to look around outside. You dish up some grub, Hagerman. Lenman, look over the barn and the corral. You, Lane, stay out in the yard."

"Rusty still wants a drink of water," Dewey said.

"Soon as I'm good and ready. The stage due today, Hagerman?"

"Yeah. Expect it when I see it."

"Hope Benecke's got no passengers." Navarro muttered.

Denial of water to the thirsty prisoner seemed a senseless brutality to Dewey, and the look he gave Navarro indicated his feelings. Like a flame catching in dry tinder, a hostility was born between them. Dewey shouldered past the lawman. Navarro grudgingly moved the inch necessary to give way.

Dewey stood near the corner of the house and watched Navarro stalk to where the nester couple stood beside their wagon. Barton was drawn erect. The woman stood close to her husband. Navarro climbed on a wheel and looked into the wagon. Rusty at the window muttered something about water, but Navarro was already pulling up the slope.

When he reached Deway, Navarro grumbled it'll be a hell of a load off my mind when I get that boy back to jail."

"He's a bad one, is he?"

Navarro stopped at the wash bench and started rolling up his sleeves. "He killed a man across the border," the deputy said. He seemed to want to talk about it. "The one he killed, his old man is a prominent Mexican, and we got extradition papers to send Rusty back to Saltillo for trial. We sent a description up the country and they nabbed him at Angelo, and me and Lenman rode up to bring him back. Wasn't for that damn flood down there, we'd have him delivered across the Rio Grande by tomorrow." He flung his hands to dry them, then wiped them on his pants leg. "I get a thousand dollars' reward for bringing him in."

He didn't say "we," Dewey noticed. Not he and Lenman. Navarro.

"Meantime, the fellow wants a drink of water. All right if I hand him a dipper through the window?"

Navarro said, "You know why he's so thirsty? I emptied his canteen last night. Learned a long time ago how to tame a prisoner and make him behave."

Mildly, Dewey remarked, "I came in thirsty the last day, myself. It's rough out there without water. Thought maybe since he's headed for a hanging anyhow, you could —"

"Let the sonofabitch spit cotton."

"Why don't you give him a drink of water?"

"Dammit, mister, you deaf?"

Dewey wasn't really sure why he had turned so persistent about this, butting in, arguing like it was some of his business. Navarro was nobody to cross. The lawman had an air of aroused viciousness that was like a bad smell. What am I picking trouble for, Dewey wondered, and changed the subject. "So they're paying you a thousand-dollar reward. They trying him in the Laredo court?"

"Saltillo, I said. Mexican court."

"Oh." Dewey's better judgment left him again. He asked through a thin smile, finding his voice brittle, "Is it worth it?"

Navarro frowned, "What'd you mean?"

"The reward. Turning an American back to a Mexican court. You know how they operate down there. He won't have a chance."

"That's his hard luck."

"I guess it is. He just didn't look so bad to me."

Here he was crossing the deputy again, without knowing why, nor quite intending to. Navarro was uncommonly suspicious, and his teeth were clenched as the big lawman closed in on Dewey, angry and violent. Then Navarro lunged at his shirt front with bent fingers. Dewey reacted with a boxer's instinct, and Navarro found his arm shunted aside by a sharp wrist blow that brought a pained grunt out of his twisted mouth.

Hagerman stood in the doorway. "It's on."

Navarro's burning stare took Dewey in from hat to boots. "That's all, right now," the big deputy said and shuffled away.

"No offense meant," Dewey said shortly. "Just don't like another man heavy-handing me. Not even the law."

Inside, Lenman inquired, "What's the trouble, Navarro?"

"Nothing. Nothing I can't handle. You set over there, Lane. I don't like my back to the door."

Lenman kept standing. "Hagerman's got four quarts of whisky in the closet."

"Well, bring one out and quit pawin' the ground about it. What'd you say, Lane?"

"I'm for it."

"It's two-bits a throw," Hagerman warned.

"It's whatever price I say, and I say it's part of the service of the stage company."

Dewey ladled a shot of water into his cup. Navarro and Lenman took theirs straight. The three stood braced for a moment, letting the hot burn bite into their caked-dust insides.

All eyes shifted back to the bottle. Dewey, as well as the others, knew there never had been such a thing in history as one drink. Navarro went friendly and expansive soon after the second. He slapped his gun holster and stalked about the table. "From the Panhandle, huh? What's up there?"

"Mostly starvation, now," Dewey said. "The cattle market wiped out most people and the drought pushed them the rest of the way over the brink. Hard times, everywhere."

The prisoner called from behind the locked door. "Navarro? How about some chili and a drink?"

"When I'm good and ready." He called the words over his shoulder, not turning, but eying Dewey. Hagerman muttered something that brought Navarro's scowl upon him.

Lenman shifted uneasily. "Anybody but me feel like another'n?"

"You got to ask? Eh, Panhandle?"

"All right."

"Sew lace on the edge of his, Lenny."

Lenman sloshed water into Dewey's drink.

They downed the whisky. Hagerman put the chili bowls on. "It's gettin' cold. Cold chili's no better than buffalo chips."

"This stuff ain't cold." Navarro fisted his mouth. "Say, Panhandle, you're right fast

34

on your feet, I noticed. Done prize fightin'?"

Dewey understood that Navarro was going to prod him, that the incident outside still rankled. And it was not what it seemed, either — the lawman was on edge about something, and this belligerence was a cover for it. Navarro moved about as Dewey finished his drink.

He eyed Navarro over the cup rim. *Damned if I haven't pitched camp in a mess here.* He saw Navarro's gaze shift, his eyes narrow. The deputy pointed. "Godamighty, look out there!" Instinctively, Dewey turned his head to the open doorway behind him, knowing his mistake a split second afterward, remembering the trick a fraction too late, whirling back instantly and trying to draw himself into a protective knot. But the swing of the deputy's boot had already started.

Navarro kicked into Dewey's groin. Dewey staggered and dropped his cup, bending double to grab at his pain. When he could raise his head to search for Navarro in the fog of nausea, the deputy and Lenman floated into his vision, their mouths slack open, watching with far-off interest a man sick the sickest way a man can be.

"You want to take off that gun and badge

a minute?" Dewey gritted.

Navarro laughed harshly. "You show up when I ain't busy and I'll accommodate ya."

Hagerman had been cursing. He wound up, "You didn't need to do that."

"He got smart with me outside. Godamighty, that sure cools 'em, don't it?" To Dewey, he added sarcastically, "Just a little horse play, Lane. We got tricks down here on the border, ain't we, Lenny? Got to educate the smart ones."

An angered reply came to Dewey's tongue, but he forced it back. There were other ways. Navarro's own. He promised himself there would also be another time, and limped to the door. Navarro chuckled and reached for the whisky bottle.

Rusty called, "How about a drink of water, Navarro?"

Dewey leaned against the wall outside. In a minute he went to the wash bench and splashed water on his face. He got a focus on things and saw the wagon in the brush. The Bartons sat like old clothes drying before the cook fire. Dewey walked slowly that way for nothing better to do. The Bartons indicated no welcome for him. He turned his course, went to the pen, circled it, and walked without direction.

Crossing a brushy patch, he came upon a

dim trail and kept walking. Downgrade led to thicker mesquite and cedar growth, and a dampish grass bottom among creek willows where seepage came up from the arroyo. He saw a movement in the thick growth, a switching motion of dark color. Then he caught the hidden outlines of the horse.

Pushing through the willows, he found the mustang was staked with a short rope. Then he caught sight of the saddle, blanket and bridle in a brush clump to the side. Hell of a place to stake a horse. Barton stepped out of the trees before Dewey was halfway back to the station yard.

The lined face was hard set. "You see anything down there?"

Wonderingly, Dewey started to say, "Just a horse." But he checked that reply. *Careful, boy. The old man doesn't like you. What kind of a damn fiesta have I latched on to here, anyhow?*

"No, sir," he said respectfully. "Why? What's down there?"

"Why, nothing. What should there be?"

"You were the one who asked."

Barton grunted. "You look kinda peaked. Sick?"

"The deputy kicked me. Down here. I feel a little groggy." Barton thought that over. "Looks like he plucked your holster, too."

"He collected all the guns."

"Mine, too. Well, come along to our camp. My wife will fix you something to eat."

In a little while, Dewey was sitting on the padded wagon seat facing the Bartons' cook fire, with a plate of frijoles and cornbread on his knee. They had traded introductions and that was all. Barton squatted near by. Mrs. Barton spooned sugar into Dewey's mug of coffee. She had not yet spoken, and when she handed him the cup their glances met full for the first time. He saw a smile brush her face again, as it had when he had first seen her gathering the bluebonnets. Now the wilted flowers were pinned to the front of her dress. Her eyes searched him deeply. He felt that she was looking for something, that here was a troubled woman. Or was she only timid as a nester wife might be around a stranger? They were a brand of women, homesteader women were, making themselves invisible with men around, same as Indian squaws. Had a way of withdrawing to nowhere, even when in sight.

Then she spoke. "He's about the age of our boy, isn't he, Joe?"

"How old are you, Lane?" Barton inquired.

"Twenty-six."

"Then he's four years older," murmured Mrs. Barton.

"Than your son?"

"Yes."

He saw her fingers tremble, but it might have come from the weight of the coffee pot. Then, because it was so unexpected in this setting of hard-up, whipped-out failures moving somewhere else, what she said next almost made him drop his plate. Mrs. Barton murmured, to herself, it seemed, but plainly, "Yes, our son. *Alter ipse amicus.*"

Staring at her, he tried to remember what it meant. Somehow she had spoken a reassurance to herself, something meaning he was their friend, an important one, like one of their own.

He pretended ignorance. "That's Comanche, isn't it?"

She smiled. "No. That's Latin. I used to be a school teacher."

She turned the smile across the fire to her husband, still sitting on his boot heels and blowing his coffee. "Until I met Joe." Barton moved uneasily. Dewey tried to think of something to say.

"I suppose a lot of Texas school teachers married ranchers. They —"

"He wasn't a cowman, then." Her smile held on. "When I married him, Joe was the manager of the best music hall in Fort Worth."

Dewey asked, "The Princess House?"

"Yes," she said. "Do you know it? But you couldn't, you're too young."

"I've heard of it. My father lived in Fort Worth when he was a boy learning the printing trade. The Princess must have been quite a place."

"The times got bad," Barton said gruffly.

Mrs. Barton's smile dimmed and died like a spent candle. She said quietly, "Everything got bad."

4

Like many a man alone in a lonesome land and long orphaned, Dewey could hardly remember when he had sat in the presence of his own father and mother. It must have been something like this, he thought. The Bartons were old enough to be his parents. He watched them, aware of his home instincts, so long submerged.

"What's your line of business, Lane?" asked Barton.

"Professional drifter." Dewey smiled. "No, not exactly that. I'm on my way to look at some land I traded for."

"Lot of us on the move nowadays," said Barton.

Before long he found himself telling them about his trade with McCall, and how he'd warned him he was being cheated.

"Maybe you won't think so when you've seen what he traded you," Barton suggested. "What name does the place go by?"

Dewey said, "El Bar."

41

Barton stepped back from the coals. He opened his mouth, closed it.

Dewey remarked, "You seem to know the place."

"Maybe I've heard of it. Don't actually know. Is it close to the Tembler outfit?"

"Hagerman said so. He said something about trouble."

Cautiously, Barton asked, "You know about Sorro, the Mexican big stick? Runs a lot of cattle across from Laredo?"

"What does that have to do with the Tembler ranch, and El Bar?"

Barton shook his head. Mrs. Barton cleared her throat. Dewey waited, and then he realized that this line of talk was at an end. Barton finally said, "I'm a stranger down here, myself. All I know is hearsay and that ain't much. . . . More coffee?"

Dewey felt good. His pain was nearly gone. He remarked, "The deputy sheriffs up there have a man locked in a room in the station. He murdered somebody. They're turning him back to Mexico on extradition."

When this brought no response, he added, "I don't know how tricky this Rusty Ferris may be, but the deputy in charge is a tricky hombre, no doubt about that. He's afraid Rusty may have friends who might try to free him."

42

Barton asked roughly, "He say that? Is that what Navarro said?"

Dewey saw Mrs. Barton frown at her husband, and then stare strangely at him. The hard-lined face was stern. "You said you didn't see anything down there." Barton twisted a thumb toward the willow thicket downgrade.

Dewey stood, flexing his saddle-stiff muscles. "Just some brush."

Barton watched him hard for a long moment. Dewey waited, thinking he knew what prodded the man. Barton, it looked like, had him a stolen saddle horse hidden out.

Lenman came toward the campfire. The deputy swayed a little as he puffed through the weeds. "You come up here, Lane. Navarro wants you to stay around the house."

Far off, north on the Road, they heard the rising racket of the stage coming. Dewey thanked the Bartons for the meal and followed Lenman to the station yard.

The stage was pulling off the Road, with the twisted Benecke sawing at the lines, when Dewey and Lenman reached the house. Hagerman came around to grab the bridles of the lead mules. Benecke made a peculiar side-winder descent to the ground. Navarro came out. Lenman moved around to the other side of the curtained hack.

Dewey viewed a blossoming of skirts, white faces, trim legs showing. Then the girls were on the ground, with much brushing at disarranged skirts and pushing at hair knots. Sensing that all the show was on the other side, Lenman came back around and whistled low. Benecke hobbled past Navarro without looking up at him. With the mules stilled, Hagerman released the bridles and edged along the traces, craning. Dewey's attention was drawn to the older girl, something to look at.

The older girl smiled at them all impartially, as if this were a reception planned in her honor. The younger seemed unimpressed, Dewey thought.

There were five men in sight, enough for an audience. Cherry moved gracefully out a couple of steps. Dewey saw her body straighten, as she squared her small shoulders, making her dress bodice swell high and round with the movement. The audience looked. In all the station yard, for a good long moment, there existed only Cherry's two breasts and the men's eyes.

Navarro shook himself out of a trance and trudged forward. "Just a minute, ma'am," touching his hat brim to Cherry.

Cherry bestowed upon the lawman a

44

trusting smile, keeping her shoulders back, and daintily touched the stray wisps of her hair. "Oh! A sheriff!"

"At your service."

No, by God, he's not, Dewey thought numbly. But Navarro took his hat clear off, then, and made as clumsy an effort to bow as Dewey had ever beheld, outside a range bull going down in shallow quicksand.

"If you young ladies will wait just a second," Navarro mumbled. "Official duties."

The new arrivals hesitated, sensing some kind of tension, or strangeness. Navarro cleared his throat. "You got a gun on you, ladies? Any weapon in your gear?"

Cherry said, "Of course not!" Her small smile was served up to all the men. If she seemed to favor the big deputy just a little with her attention, Dewey thought that was natural. Navarro was plainly the top hand here. Cherry added, "I'm Cherry, she's May The Gibbons Sisters." She cut her eyes, batted her lashes, and changed her small leather bag to her other hand.

"The Gibbons Sisters" was supposed to mean something, because when there was no immediate response, Cherry puckered up a tiny frown, but the smile stayed engraved.

Benecke had his moment. "Them are show girls."

"No." Cherry tossed her head. "We're singers. Vocalists. We sing duets. May and I. That's *all*."

The younger sister spoke. Very calm and contained, Dewey noticed. Not trying as hard as the other to make the big white buttons on her bosom front stand out. Not that she needed to. "We have an engagement to sing at the Laredo Lady."

"That's where we're from. Laredo." Navarro indicated himself and Lenman. "Guess we'll be seeing you in town."

"You'll probably be needin' a little protection," Lenman said, "if you're singin' at the Lady."

Benecke snapped to Hagerman, "Let's get these mules in the pen. When did the creek stampede?"

Navarro turned on the driver. "Carry the ladies' bags inside, Benecke."

"Do it yourself, Navarro!" Benecke shot back. "I got work to do with these mules."

Cherry murmured, "Shall we go inside, May?"

May said thinly, "If you're ready."

Navarro found his manners again. "Come right in!" He made a grand motion, and the girls moved past. He said, "We got a pris-

46

oner locked up inside. But nothing for you to worry about."

Dewey saw Cherry turn back. "A prisoner! Here in this house? My goodness!"

May Gibbons glanced reflectively around the man circle again as if seeking to get identities straightened out. Dewey reached for the valise she carried. Their hands came together on the handle. "I can manage," she said.

He smiled his insistence and carried the bag. He heard Navarro expound further about the desperate qualities of his prisoner and his own dangerous and important responsibilities. Then the group unfroze and movement flowed again, carrying them into the long dim room.

Depositing May's valise on the floor, Dewey eased outside and picked a seat on the wash bench. He heard Navarro's talk and occasional chatty words from Cherry. Hagerman and Benecke went around the corner with the stage team. Lenman sauntered in and out, rifle under his arm, and when he went in he gave Dewey a broad wink, as if here was something for their mutual appreciation. The younger girl, May Gibbons, came to the doorway once and looked out. Dewey saw that she avoided a direct glance at him.

Navarro evidently was making the second bedroom available to the girls, the small cubicle adjoining Rusty's cell. Dewey heard him genially tell them to move right in and not be afraid if they saw a scorpion or two. "We're apt to be caught here another twenty-four hours."

Hagerman returned from the pen. Soon, from the smell inside, Dewey knew that he was heating up chili for the new arrivals. Cherry Gibbons came out and expressed a desire to walk down and see the flooded Cibolo.

Navarro made a benevolent hand motion. "We want you folks to pass the time just any old way that suits you. Mosey around and take it easy, and me and Lenman will look after things. We don't want to cramp nobody's style. Just remember we got a bad man on our hands and a responsibility to hold him. Extradition case. Governor's extradition, got the signed papers right on me, Governor Richard Coke himself. There's a murderer in that room and we ain't allowin' for him to pull no surprise. Not till we turn him over to the law across the border. Now you folks don't worry about a thing. Fact, I was going down to see the creek myself, and I'll be glad to escort the two young ladies if you want to see it."

48

Navarro wound up his speech with his eyes on Cherry. She gave the deputy a bold, responding smile. "Come on, May. Let's go with Mr. Navarro and see the creek."

The younger sister, Dewey saw, was holding back. Dewey took in again May's smooth-tanned cheeks, the small patch of nose freckles, the way her dark braids had loosened from the jolting stage ride, the two big white buttons on her dress front. Her dress matched the one Cherry wore, and it occurred to him that he should visit the Laredo Lady sometime. May's slight figure stood erect, poised, agile. She showed a seasoning of distrust, this one, or a younger sister's strain at independence.

Navarro and Cherry walked toward the creek, with Cherry chatting easily, cocking her head up to the deputy. Dewey thought of asking May to walk with him, sensing a timidness or uncertainty in her. Better leave her alone. Sure enough, he thought, this one was just a singing show girl and that *was* all.

Dewey walked to the creek with Lenman. When he looked back to find May, before they entered the brushy down slope, she was walking aimlessly across the station yard, in the general direction of the nesters' camp.

The group stood on the arroyo edge and watched the murky water roll below. The creek still fussed and caroused on its way to oblivion in the Gulf far off. The drift sign told Dewey it was slowly falling.

The dirty flow was something more than just a stream to be crossed, he thought. It was something that held up all these people for a time, himself included, until some highly personal decisions and purposes could be forded, too. The road on the other side stretched south and out of sight. The Cibolo churned there, a trap beginning to relax its grip as the waters fell. "Maybe by tomorrow," Dewey said, "this thing will turn us loose."

Cherry repeated absently, "Tomorrow."

Navarro and Cherry walked on a little distance, and Dewey heard the word "tomorrow" again in fragments of their own conversation.

This was sure enough a *mañana* crowd, he thought. All on account of a cloudburst maybe a hundred miles away. Trouble was, there was a night of being crowded together in this place standing between them all and their individual *mañanas.*

Dewey returned to the station yard alone and caught sight of the nester's wagon. He remembered the horse and saddle gear hidden in the willow thicket. Bound to be stolen. Otherwise there was no sense to

50

staking a horse in a place like that. All at once he remembered how the prisoner had glanced at the Barton camp when he had first arrived. Something in Rusty's expression, the quick way he had dropped his glance. Did that hook up some way, Dewey wondered, with the hidden horse?

Inside the 'dobe, in the dim cool shadows of the long main room, he got a cup of coffee from Hagerman. May Gibbons came in. She hesitated, glancing across at Dewey with a level look, then headed for the small room where the girls' suitcases stood on the floor. He saw her profile turn briefly toward the adjoining locked door. Hagerman had lined three cots along the wall of the main room. Dewey, watching the younger sister, indicated them. "You'll have lots of body-guards, but not much privacy."

"We've stayed in stranger places." She marched into the small room and gently closed the door.

Cherry Gibbons came in swiftly, with her face flushed pink, her mouth hard set. Navarro crowded behind her in the middle of saying something but, seeing Dewey, the deputy cut it off. His eyes turned brittle, revealing the kind of hunger that ate him and why Cherry Gibbons had a flushed face and a grim mouth. Navarro floundered, muttered something, and went outside.

"A drink of water!" Cherry tried to make her voice gay, failed to quite achieve it. "I'm famished. Isn't the creek something to see?"

Dewey handed her a filled dipper. She drank, taking time to compose herself. "I guess the Laredo Lady can wait until we get there. It's part of trouping, you know. Where's my little sister?"

"In your room." Dewey saw her face lose its attempted gaiety as Cherry looked at both closed doors at the end of the long room. He saw the shadows under her makeup. The girl is carrying a load of trouble, Dewey thought. Packed up out of sight, but there just the same.

"You must come see our act sometime," Cherry said.

"I'd like to see your act," he murmured. "Your other one."

He saw the slow, comprehending change of her expression. She tried to cover her confusion with a defiant lift of her head, then turned her back on him and fled to her room.

Benecke hobbled in. He cocked a shrewd eye up to Dewey. "Understand you got the Laredo law greeting. Hagerman told me."

"Told you what?"

"Navarro. The sonofabitch and his kickin'

stunt." Benecke glanced down at his twisted hip. "Be glad he didn't stomp you."

Navarro loomed in the doorway behind Benecke. Dewey frowned a warning to the crippled driver.

Navarro had heard, however. "Be damn careful, Benecke, or I'll —"

Benecke whirled. "You'll what? What else can be done to me that ain't already done? You ask him, stranger — ask the dirty sonofabitch how I got this way. Ask him — !"

Dewey saw the crazed anger, the defiance of the crippled little man, the way he hunkered before Navarro like a mortally hurt animal.

"All right, Benecke, I'll ask him." Dewey looked steadily at the deputy. "How did Benecke get that way? What happened to him, Navarro?"

The deputy shifted his anger from Benecke to Dewey. Hagerman, working at the counter, turned and silently slid the long-bladed butcher knife down the planks almost to where Dewey's hand rested on the counter edge. Navarro's mouth corners hardened into knots.

"The trouble-maker." He placed a heavy; hand on his gun holster. "You landed here making trouble. I should have kicked your guts out, learned you a lesson —"

Dewey's hand closed on the knife handle. "You want to try it again, Navarro?"

Benecke limped aside. Hagerman stood bull-heavy in his tracks. The intervening six paces between Dewey and Navarro loomed empty and open.

Dewey waited, feeling nothing, holding Navarro's eye, alert to the man's next move. From across the table Benecke whispered harshly, "This one's your size. Try stompin' *him!*"

Navarro stared with whiskey-eyed hatred at Dewey. His fingers slid to the gun handle. In that moment, the far door squeaked and Cherry Gibbons came out.

"Later!" Navarro muttered.

"I smell food!" Cherry exclaimed.

She stopped. Her eyes settled to Navarro with his hand on his gun, to Dewey, his hand on the long knife on the counter. May Gibbons entered, almost bumping into her sister.

Hagerman was the first to move. "Dinner's ready."

Navarro turned as if in pain and walked out.

Cherry Gibbons's taco had turned harshly sober. She leveled on Dewey. "I'd like to see *your* act, too!"

"I'm not much of a performer. Maybe you

could teach me."

"You do all right."

Dewey walked to the door, and Cherry murmured as he passed, "Thank you."

He nodded, not correcting her. He knew that Cherry assumed that he had been in trouble with Navarro over her honor, over the pass Navarro obviously had been fumbling to make. Wandering toward the crossing again, he smiled at her acceptance of him as a guardian of female honor.

The creek was still lowering itself, and he hoped that if the fall continued through the night he would be able to swim his horse over sometime tomorrow. Maybe before another sunset he would be cutting the black's tracks into his own deeded earth, El Bar.

5

Night came over the Laredo Road.

The lamps burned in the stage station and at the wagon camp down the slope the cook fire lapped red for a while, then died.

At the supper table, in the early dusk, the conversation of the travelers floundered and then came to an uneasy pause, like a coyote nosing around for a forgotten hiding place. It might have been on everyone's mind that Rusty Ferris, who had been fed alone, earlier, was just beyond the locked door and could hear every word that was said.

Hagerman had dished out a salty beef stew. Seven steaming plates of it on the table made a lot of smell. The air of the room became so laden with the greasy steaming odor that a deep breath was almost a meal in itself.

Navarro had stew juice dribbling his chin and his calculating eyes mostly hung to what showed of Cherry Gibbons between the table edge and her neck. Lenman, who evidently had hit the whisky again, tried to think of cute, rawhiding things to say for the pleasure of the girls.

Dewey could see the darkening sky through the open doorway. Before they had finished the meal a scattering of stars smeared the sky.

Navarro told them again how they would sleep. "Me and Lenman out here, so's we can keep an eye on him. With Lane. You girls in your room, Hagerman and Benecke at the barn. Don't nobody move around sudden during the night."

"We goin' to take turns sittin' up, Blackie?" Lenman asked.

"We'll just doze with one ear open. Rusty ain't going nowhere."

Navarro pushed his chair back. He remembered something.

"You girls're singers." He made a slack grin while he rolled a cigarette. "How about giving us a little sample? Little idea of what we'll hear at the Laredo Lady?"

"Yeah, do that!" Lenman beamed.

"Oh — we couldn't!" Cherry protested. "No piano music — it wouldn't be the same without music and costumes and everything."

"Aw, go on! Stand over there and give us a tune. Little dance with it, maybe?"

Hagerman croaked unexpectedly, "Yeah. I'd like to hear a song. Never get to town."

Navarro licked his cigarette. "What'd you say — Dewey Lane?"

Lenman broke in with a cackle. "Dewey Lane! That's a funny name. Like a wet road. Get it?"

"He looks a little dry to me."

"He needs a drink, Blackie. We all need a drink!"

"I'll get it. I saw the bottle," May Gibbons said.

"Handy girl to have around," said Lenman. "Knows when a man needs a drink." Navarro kept ragging Cherry for a song.

May brought three tin cups. "This was all. Unless there's another bottle somewhere."

"Another'n the closet," said Lemnan.

She extended a cup to Dewey, then placed the others before Navarro and Lenman.

"God, this is a real slug!" Lenman said.

"Way I like it!" Navarro retorted.

Dewey found his own drink watered weak. May hadn't distributed the whisky very evenly.

"What about that song?" Navarro started again. "Let's hear you sing something." He gulped down his drink, a long one.

"All right, May. Let's try it." Cherry moved out from the table, backing up near the bedroom doors. May came to stand beside her. Both fumbled nervously with their hands, then seemed to get hold of their professional poise.

"Sing something with a little pepper in it," Lenman called.

Navarro laughed. "Make old Rusty in there dance in his handcuffs — cheer him up a little."

Cherry felt of her throat and appeared to think hard. "A lively one is hard to do without a piano. I think we'll try something with slower harmony. A ballad."

"There's a new one." May spoke tonelessly to the table circle of lifted faces. "We learned it at Angelo."

"Oh, yes — that's my choice!" Cherry said quickly. "*Chula Chalita.*"

They experimented with their tone and pitch, and started. Dewey heard the first notes of Cherry's clear lead, May's soft alto, and knew that their voices really were not good. Not too bad, maybe, but not good. But the tune itself was strangely appealing — a wistful melody, softly sung, haunting, like a night prairie or a dim line of Mexican hills.

Mañana comes soon . . . so soon . . .
   so soon . . .
So kiss me once again, Chula Chalita.
I love you true . . . be true . . . be true . . .
Mañana comes soon, Chula Chalita.

59

When the new day breaks, the desert
  grows light,
Give me your love, now, so swift is the
  night.

Mañana must be, say *sí* . . . say *sí* . . .
See the sun stealing near, Chula Chalita.
Whisper in the night . . . tonight . . . this
  night . . .
Dream of this night *mañana,* my Chula
  Chalita . . .

The applause by Navarro and Lenman
was boisterous, from the others, perfunc-
tory. Cherry laughed self-consciously and
cried, "Oh, it would have been much better
with piano music." May continued to wear
the slight frown she had put on while trying
to cope with her husky harmony.

In a moment of stillness that followed the
applause, a footstep on a creaking board
sounded from the locked room behind the
girls.

Navarro threw his head back and bellowed, "How'd you like that, Rusty?"

Cherry looked tired. She ran her hand over
her eyes. "Now, if you will excuse us . . ."

Over Lenman's thick-tongued protests
that they should encore, the Gibbons sisters
said good night, went to their room and

closed the door. Dewey finished his drink, a weak one to start, and a meager one.

"Not bad singers," Benecke commented. "Pretty song. What's that 'Chula Chalita'?"

"Means something like 'dear little one,' I think," Dewey said.

"Get this mess cleaned up, Hagerman!" Navarro struggled to his feet. "We got to sleep with this smell?"

"All you smell is whisky," Hagerman grunted.

The blackness outside closed down. After a time Dewey and the two lawmen selected their cots in the long room. Hagerman and Benecke headed for the barn.

Eventually, with the lamps out, Lenman, swaying beside his cot, stared a long moment at the closed door of the girls' room. Navarro worked his boots off with a noticeable struggle, and Dewey speculated that first and last the pair of them had taken on a skinful of whisky. The distant surge of the troubled Cibolo came in faintly, reminding Dewey of what Hagerman had told him, that it made him think of how Indians sounded, attacking at dawn.

For a time each bunk in the house seemed to have rocks in it that were slow to dissolve under uneasy flesh. The station room shouted chili peppers, boiled beef, whisky, body sweat and horses. Putting out the last lamp turned it all loose in the blackness, and the odors became a dirty rat-nosed animal of the night on the prowl. But they slept at last, those who snored doing so as naturally as if they were old friends or long married.

Once, during the night, fitfully awake, Dewey peered at the girls' door and remembered Lenman trying to see through. The half-asleep vision he had of Cherry was born of long miles on a womanless road. From his cot, his glance shifted in the darkness to Rusty Ferris's locked door. Must be torture, wearing handcuffs all day and then having to sleep in them at night. Then his sleepy thoughts strayed to what he might find at his El Bar land and if he would be seeing it by the next afternoon. This substitute did not entirely succeed, for Cherry Gibbons's expression of mixed anxiety and gay boldness kept intruding, and this little duel of his half-dreams kept up until Dewey finally slept again.

Navarro looked shaky and red-eyed in the first light of morning. "You must have slugged me with that last drink," he said jokingly to May.

"I'm not a very good bartender, I guess."

"You'll do. When I want a drink, I want a *drink!*"

They finished breakfast and were in a general move toward the door, all anxious to see what the crossing looked like this day.

May Gibbons walked over to Dewey. She looked at him as if she had been deliberating for weeks over something important to tell him. He remembered this later, because it was practically the first time the matter-of-fact younger sister had spoken directly to him. But all she actually said was, "It's a beautiful morning out, isn't it? — or offers to be."

"It does," said Dewey. He saw that just that amount of intimacy, if it could be called such, had turned her uncommonly tense, or something had. Her lips actually trembled. He smiled straight down to the dark face. "Right pretty morning."

"I'll bring my boy out and feed and water him," Navarro grunted. He worked the key from his pocket and advanced to Rusty's door.

Lenman leaned against the side wall, looking as bleary-eyed and hung-over as Navarro. Dewey turned back, pulled with a curiosity to see Rusty Ferris again. He noticed May Gibbons move a few steps closer to Cherry. Cherry seemed to be drawn taut as a wire and pale white in the shadowy dawn.

Navarro fumbled with the key in the lock.

"All right, Rusty," he said, whisky-hoarse. "I'm goin' to feed you now. Come meet the wimmin."

May whispered audibly, "I don't want to see this!"

Navarro threw the door back.

Hagerman had stopped his chores, turning to watch from the far end of the room. Benecke stood in his hip-shot huddle. Dewey, sighting them each in turn, sensed the tension, felt it spreading.

Navarro stepped into the dim shadows of Rusty's room.

When Navarro reappeared he came with his pants seat first, retreating with high-lifted steps like a person who has nearly stepped on a snake. Dewey noticed, puzzled, that the visible part of Navarro's neck had turned from brown to white. Navarro grunted an unintelligible sound. Now he was all the way out, past the door, still walking backward. As he moved with slow steps, his back to the room, his heavy elbows began to spread out until his forearms floated upward and his hands dangled limply on either side of his head.

Rusty came into sight, slow, following

Navarro, and holding the butt of a big black revolver raised belly-high in his two hands. The big dark hole in the old Colt's heavy muzzle centered on Navarro's muscle-breasted chest. The sleek black hammer was cocked all the way back.

May's beautiful morning hung still and ugly. Dewey held his breath. The prisoner's thin, fuzzy face was strained like an old man's, twisted with his tension and with his gamble.

Navarro's voice boomed out accusingly, "He's got a gun!"

Benecke breathed the same words, and Lenman was muttering them, too, until they all had said what they saw, as if it might have been overlooked. He had a gun.

He was only coming out to breakfast, or should have been. It was supposed to have been a little item of interest for everybody, and then they could go look at the crossing. It wasn't supposed to be like this, but it was.

Rusty came on and Navarro kept backing. Dewey tried to see Navarro better, and stayed paralyzed like the others, hoping that Navarro didn't move wrong. There was no telling who Rusty would start pulling the trigger on in those close quarters if some-body stampeded. Navarro backed past the table after first bumping into the end of it, jerked nervously, and then edged around. Rusty kept coming, beginning now a side drift toward the outside door, his manacled hands holding the gun out in front of him.

Dewey was nearest to the door, nearest in Rusty's way of exit, and he moved aside, very carefully, knowing that Rusty watched him without taking his eyes off Navarro.

At no time did Rusty say a word, or take his gaze off Navarro, which now included Lenman in the same line of sight, Lenman with mouth hung open and his rifle leaned against the wall.

Rusty made the door. He risked one quick look outside behind him. He risked another quick look at everybody in the room in turn, to Navarro with his arms raised, to Lenman shrunk into the wall beside his carbine, and last to the girls.

Then he was out the door. He ducked to one side of the door facing. View of him was cut off from the room. They breathed again.

Navarro crouched and drew his gun. Lenman grabbed the carbine. He and Navarro collided with each other in a mix-up going around the table. Navarro headed for the door, his gun up, and this time Cherry Gibbons moved out and there was further confusion as Cherry bumped into Navarro. Dewey felt a soft touch, looked down and saw that May had grabbed his arm. Navarro clumsily side-stepped Cherry, dropped low to the floor and peered around the door edge.

"He's headed for the horses!"

Navarro straightened and rushed outside. Lenman hurried after him. Dewey and the other men made a cautious exit, and once in the yard they lost sight of both Navarro and Lenman, who rounded the house corner.

Dewey thought of the window in the north side, from where he could see the corral, and rushed into the house, across to the small opening. He sighted Rusty at once, running backward, the sixgun still raised in his two hands.

A Colt blasted twice, out of Dewey's sight. Rusty kept running backward. Now he turned, ran with his back toward the house for a few paces, and whirled to see the yard again, still running. Lenman's carbine spat and the bullet whined off with a dirt spray beside Rusty's running boots.

Rusty paused, the gun steadied, bucked, and the roar rattled the window where Dewey watched. Rusty aimed and the gun in his hands smoked again.

Dewey heard the little cry of one of the girls close behind him. He turned to find Cherry and May crowding at his shoulder, straining to see, their faces drained white. He whirled back. Rusty was disappearing around the corner of the pen, toward the cedar brush. Somebody outside was yelling orders. Navarro, probably. A gun boomed again. There was no further sound from Lenman's carbine.

Rusty vanished into the growth behind the corral. Dewey slipped past the girls and went to the yard and saw Benecke and Hagerman standing near the corner, looking down at something beyond and out of sight. Dewey joined them.

Navarro was there, gun in hand. He jogged a little way toward the pen, looked undecided, and jogged back. He had all the earmarks of a man badly rattled, as he had a right to be. And last night's whisky was not helping. Lenman lay on his side on the ground, stretched in a thin bundle with his knees drawn up toward his belt. Dewey saw why the carbine hadn't stopped Rusty. Lenman was dead.

Navarro looked down at Lenman's bloody head, and then leaned against the 'dobe wall, took off his hat, wiped his forehead, replaced his hat, pulled at his yellow scarf to get more throat air, blew his nose to one side, still holding the Colt in that hand, and cursed.

He straightened, walked stiff-legged past the others, giving a dazed look down at Lenman as he went past the crumpled body.

"Break out the guns, Hagerman!" Navarro called. "All of you get a gun. We got to ride in that brush and get him."

Hagerman went inside. The girls came to the doorway and no farther.

Benecke bent over Lenman, then he hobbled away toward the pen, saw what he looked for, and hurried back. "All the stock's been let out of the pen, Navarro."

The deputy blinked his dull comprehension.

Hagerman brought out the assortment of guns. Navarro muttered, "Damn little use, now." Navarro seemed to have forgotten that Lenman lay out there dead. He looked darkly off toward the brush. "There went a thousand dollars."

The only four-footed stock left on the place were the Bartons' wagon team, staked near their camp. It took Hagerman and Benecke, riding these, till mid-afternoon to round up the animals that had scattered and strayed in all directions — the stage mules and extra horses, Dewey's black, the three horses the lawmen and Rusty had ridden. Navarro's pursuit of his prisoner came to an end before it ever got started.

Down in the trees, Dewey could see Mr. and Mrs. Barton. Barton had come upgrade, once, to see what all the trouble was about, and had helped Hagerman and Benecke untie his two mustangs to go on their search for the horses.

Navarro came to the doorway, trailing a new whisky bottle by its neck. Thickly, he said to Dewey, "I just want to know who done it. That's all. Who got the gun to him and who let the horses out of the pen last night."

"He foxed you, Deputy," Hagerman commented.

"Not yet, he ain't. Not with those handcuffs still on."

He turned around unsteadily and went back into the station.

"The tracks down there." Hagerman brought it up to Dewey, what they had seen in their search below the pen. "How did he do it? No man can put a bridle on a horse when his hands are fastened together."

"You thought of that, too? It might could be done, if he'd had practice and time, and if the horse would co-operate."

"Easier, though," said Hagerman, "if done for him."

"Well, he could have had a pal or two out here last night. Maybe he belonged to an

70

outlaw gang." Dewey kept his mouth shut about the hidden horse, saddle and bridle in the willows.

When late afternoon came, the people at the side of the Laredo Road were quiet and avoided going near Navarro, who was inside, the chase abandoned, still engaged in getting himself drunk. They all agreed the creek would be down, and a fording possible, by morning.

Cherry and May Gibbons wandered in the yard and finally wound up at the wagon camp, where they could be seen talking with the Bartons. Hagerman and Benecke were digging a grave for Lenman in the softer ground east of the pen, and Dewey went over to spell them with the spade and pick.

Navarro came to the corner, lifting his dark head for a blurred, bullish look over things. He sighted the burial work and headed that way, trailing the whisky bottle by its neck like a dead hen. Something seemed to have burned into his brain, a purpose, or a delayed duty, from the way he came hard on at the group.

He came to a weaving halt, confronting Dewey. "You're under arrest, Lane. Material witness."

"That's crazy, Navarro. I —"

"You're goin' to jail till I work out this

case, what happened here —"

"You're drunk!"

"Somebody helped Rusty pull this — I want to know more about you — where you —"

"I had nothing to do with Rusty's escape. You know it."

Navarro licked his lips. All at once the deputy actually looked sober, and in a way that Dewey did not like. Navarro took a deep breath and placed the whisky bottle on the ground. "You're under arrest."

Dewey had restored his Colt to its holster when Hagerman had brought out all the weapons soon after Rusty's escape. When Navarro advanced, Dewey stood in his tracks, watching to see what the man intended to do.

Navarro said, "I'll take that gun off you."

"Not this time."

Navarro lunged at him. Dewey side-stepped, twisted, and scraped Navarro's gun from its holster, all in one flash of move-ment. Navarro slapped at his empty holster too late. His expression tightened. He came at Dewey again, in slow, animal-like stalk-ing. "I'm still takin' you prisoner, mister."

Dewey wouldn't, and couldn't, shoot the man in cold blood. He also realized that Navarro knew this. Yet the man was forcing him to act, one way or another. He could not understand why. Then Benecke spoke from the edge of the half-finished grave, and it was explanation enough.

"Mad and drunk and women watching. Got to beat up *somebody.*"

Navarro paid no attention to Benecke. He kept coming. Dewey kept retreating warily. Hagerman muttered, "Look out, Lane."

Benecke warned, "He'll stomp you if he gets you down!"

Dewey was tired of backing around the grave in a circle. The extra gun in his hand was a nuisance, and to get rid of it, knowing no better place, he flung it into the loose dirt of the grave without taking his eyes off Navarro. Benecke reached in and retrieved it.

Then, because it would only be in his way in this kind of trouble, Dewey quickly un-buckled his own gunbelt and flung it out, holstered gun and all, toward Benecke. "Hold that for me."

In the same moment Navarro swarmed in. The rush had weight and surprising foot agility behind it. Navarro smashed so quick into him that Dewey failed his side-step by inches. Navarro's powerful shoulder caught him a swipe in the ribs and he stumbled backward, lost footing in a mound of loose dirt, and went sprawling boots over head into the shallow grave opening. The fall all but knocked the wind out of him. He fought for air in his lungs as he twisted catlike, looking up, just in time to see Navarro poised for the jump.

Navarro jumped straight down upon him, feet first. Dewey saw the boots coming, twisted in the narrow confines of the opening, and barely threshed aside before Navarro's weight could crush his chest. This threw the deputy off balance, and Dewey shoved him sprawling, then rolled out and off across the dirt clods. He was struggling to his feet when Navarro came puffing hard up out of the grave.

He came at Dewey again, stepping over Lenman's quilt-wrapped body.

This time Dewey was ready for his rush. But just as he side-stepped, delivering a right uppercut toward Navarro's jaw, the deputy halted his rush, inches short. Navarro aimed a fist, and a grin with it for the way he had fooled Dewey. Barely ducking the blow that grazed his ear and felt as if it had taken his ear off, Dewey got set again, trying to organize himself a little. He tried Navarro with a flashing straight fist that connected with his cheekbone. The dark face hardly gave and Dewey's fist felt as if he had struck a flintrock wall. He knew that the weight and the power of the man would be almost impossible to beat down.

Navarro's mouth hung slack and wet as he came in, fists flailing, any one of his swinging blows powerful enough to flatten a man. Dewey retreated, dodging and weaving the best he could. Navarro leaned forward, back, and his boot toe flew up, hard and high. Dewey was ready for that, and doubled up, at the same time grabbing blindly at the big man's boot. It was an awkward grab, but all at once he had boot toe and heel in his hands, locked tight as a vise. His luck was fool's luck, but once he had it, he played it with cagey deliberation. He held on to the boot, twisting, and Navarro struggled and danced on one foot until he lost balance and had to go down. Not yet did Dewey release his hold. His muscles put all the power he could into the twist. He felt the ankle give, raglike. Navarro grunted loudly, and kicked crazily at Dewey's hand with his free boot. Blood showed as he kicked the skin loose, battering Dewey's fingers. But Dewey held his bloody grip, twisting with all the weight and power of his shoulders.

He tossed Navarro's foot aside, saw Navarro immediately start a frenzied scramble to get up, and knew what would happen. Navarro made his feet, started a rush, and his twisted ankle gave way. As he almost fell, Dewey hit him. His knuckles cracked solidly into Navarro's left eye. He slammed again into Navarro's stomach, his right again to the throat, and Navarro went hobbling backward. Dewey pounced fast after him, gulping for breath, trying to see through dirt-smeared eyes, beating Navarro with everything he could throw, fists battering Navarro in the face and stomach and neck. The deputy staggered, shook his head and tried to shield it with thick bent arms. Then he made a stumbling rush, grabbing and holding Dewey who tried to batter his way free.

It had been a mistake to let Navarro get him at close quarters. Navarro loosened one hand, his big right fist worked low, and Dewey was lifted in a burst of pain where Navarro smashed him low in the groin. Navarro's weight was overwhelming. The last blow made him stomach sick, then sick all over. Navarro was going to do it again. Dewey twisted, got his right arm free, and plunged a thumb stab into Navarro's already closed left eye. Navarro fell back. Dewey side-stepped, weak from his hurt, and stumbled.

Navarro rushed, sprang into the air, came

down with both feet stiffly extended, his boot heels aimed for Dewey's face. Dewey did not quite jerk from under. One boot missed. But the heel of the other plowed a furrow across the side of his head, a strip of blood spurting out, a white-hot flash of pain blinding him. The whole side of his head went numb,and he fought back with savage intensity, thinking Navarro had blinded him. Navarro, who had followed the stomping attempt by falling hard upon Dewey, was slower now, showing some effects from the fist battering he had taken. As Dewey fought him off with fists and knees, he rolled from under the killing weight, flipped aside, and fought dizzily to his feet.

Navarro came up from the dirt with one arm oddly bent behind him. Dewey caught the wolf cunning suddenly showing in Navarro's one good eye, but he only had time to think of hitting Navarro in his bloodied face while the man was still off balance. He bore in, arms pumping, feeling like dead weights on his shoulders but staggering Navarro. Navarro moved sluggishly, floundered, shook his head sleepily, then made one last try. A Navarro kind of try, and Benecke yelped and Hagerman bellowed something, but it was too late to help Dewey. Navarro's bent right arm came around, and he had the neck of the whisky bottle in his fist, the bottle his hand had closed upon as he had come up off the ground. Dewey saw it coming, too late. This bottle was almost full, and Navarro swung with all his remaining force. The bottle crashed on Dewey's bare temple and felled him in a shower of glass. . . .

It seemed a long time later when he heard, far off, a voice say, "Nope. No stompin' him, Navarro. I got this gun on you. . . ." Benecke's voice? He didn't have time to decide. Blackness washed in again as if he were being covered up in Lenman's grave.

6

Navarro stayed indoors at Laredo the first two days after his troubles at the stage station, alone with his hurts, his hangover and his moody hatred for a man named Dewey Lane. As the law of Laredo, he had a pride, a vanity in looking the part, and he was chief supporter of the local legend that no man had ever whipped Blackie Navarro.

Riding toward the jail office now, Blackie's worries churned with thoughts of his two bosses, Pete Sorro on the Mexican side and Jake Tembler on the north. The matter of losing Rusty Ferris was an unfortunate thing. During those two days of waiting for his bruised eye to open, Blackie brooded that the trouble not only had cost him a thousand dollars but was sure to ignite Sorro's wrath as well. Mike Sorro, the bandit's son, had been overdue for killing, considering what a polecat kind of a show-off he was, and Navarro secretly felt satisfaction that Rusty Ferris had done the job when the swaggering Mike had tried to knife the gringo hired hand. But that didn't keep Papa Sorro from demanding the capture of Rusty Ferris, first to be hanged by the thumbs and later to be stood before a firing squad of his outlaws. It had been Navarro's job to find Ferris and smuggle him across the border for torture and death.

With Rusty Ferris lost, Navarro began speculation on how he might scheme the substitution of Dewey Lane as somebody to appease Sorro. Suppose he delivered Lane across the border to Sorro, made his admission to Sorro that Rusty Ferris had got away but offered Lane as Rusty's pal who had engineered the escape? What Sorro mostly wanted, Navarro thought, was a good drunken orgy and firing-squad excitement, as appeasement to his crazed vengeance for the death of young Mike.

In the early morning quiet, the deputy walked his horse along the back streets, thinking of the things he had to do, and with a bad taste in his mouth for all of them. Among the first would be the need to report to Sorro and Tembler, to learn what might have been planned during his absence for the next delivery by Sorro's outfit to Tembler's range. Sorro, he knew, had been lately raiding both sides of the river to complete a herd of two hundred horses that Tembler had contracted to the Army, somewhere in the north, at a hundred dollars a head. It would be Navarro's job to clear the river fording and discourage chance witnesses when the time came to cross the herd into Texas.

As long as the Rangers and the Border Patrol were too thin in numbers to give attention to politics in far-off Laredo, Navarro owned himself a town and knew it.

In 1875, the river bank section of Laredo was a hodgepodge of squat adobe houses, sheltering maybe half the border town's claim to three thousand inhabitants. Each hovel in the Mexican quarter averaged under its roof a peon, his four or five nearly naked, brown offspring and his woman.

Sheriff Haze Trevino ran for office every two years. according to law. The minority "white" side of town, north of the Mexican quarter, was now complaining openly that Trevino never sobered long enough to even know that there had been an election. They said Blackie Navarro came in each time with the Mexicans' ballots and informed Trevino that he had won. Navarro, with some of the peons' own blood in his veins because a part-white, part-Spanish father had sired him in the very same settlement, attended to the details. He told the leaders when to distribute the ballot slips, the way to mark them, and picked up the ballot boxes on election night. He had an Apache method for handling a rare dissenter when he got him alone in a cell. Trevino kept getting elected. Pete Sorro and Jake Tembler saw that Navarro and Trevino got their rewards out of the arrangement.

When he entered the jail, acutely conscious of his battered features, Navarro found Sheriff Trevino, for a miracle, in the office. Trevino was an overweight, balding man with protruding white eyes that glazed over when he got his whisky load on, usually by early afternoon.

"Heard yesterday," Trevino murmured. "How did it happen?"

Navarro put his boots to the desk top and bit off a cheroot tip. "I don't want a lot of damn questions. We lost our prisoner. Lenman got killed. That's all."

"Too bad," Trevino sighed. "You got no trace of the boy? He get clean away?"

No use telling Trevino that he had been wool-minded from whisky when it happened, that he had damned sure had no intention of going singlehanded and afoot into the thick brush looking for Rusty Ferris.

Not with Lenman already dead and those others at the station acting like they were more for the prisoner than for Navarro. He only grunted, "Clean away."

"Why didn't you use your gun on him somewhere along the road?"

"Because Sorro wanted him delivered alive. How'd you hear about it?"

"People came in on the stage, they told it around. Blackie, Pete Sorro's not going to like it, you losing the boy."

"Nobody said he would."

"I'm just mentionin' it."

"You don't need to."

"By God, I'm the sheriff, Blackie!"

"Yeah, you're the sheriff. The dressed-up bag of lard with the star on your coat. You're the sheriff but I'm the *law* in Laredo, and don't you ever forget it."

"Hell, Blackie, no use havin' an argument over nothing."

"Over nothing! Damn it, I'm the one that keeps us in office and takes care of the Mexican vote and does the work with Sorro and Tembler. And now get to hell out — you're in my way."

Trevino mustered what remnants of dignity he could and padded to the door. "Hate to mention this, Blackie. But Jake Tembler's had word that somebody is taking over the

El Bar claim again. He wants that place himself."

"Anything else?"

"Why, yeah, there is. The Citizens Committee sent a couple of business men to call on me and ask a question. Old Ed Carlos, the editor, asked me the same thing. Carlos is gettin' to be right nosy."

"What was the damned question?"

"The white man you had in the back cell a couple of weeks ago. The drunk from some place. Name of Davis." Trevino dropped his voice. "The one you pistol-whipped pretty bad."

"What did they want to know?"

"Doc Orr put it out that he died. From the pistol-whipping."

Navarro frowned. "Well, did he?"

Sheriff Trevino hitched at his silver-plated gun butt and prepared to depart. "He sure did, Blackie. He sure as hell died on me while you were gone."

Navarro thought that over and liked it so little he put it out of his mind for something else. "Tembler's report that somebody's bought the McCall claim — he didn't hear the name Dewey Lane mentioned, did he?"

"No. Who's he?"

"Nobody," Navarro said absently, "just a guy from the Panhandle, said he was down here to look at some land he'd traded for."

Later that morning, Navarro gave some instructions to his assistant, Deputy Gomez. "I want you to do a little checking around town. On this Rusty Ferris trouble. I don't look much like getting out yet."

"You sure don't," Gomez agreed. "Maybe Ferris had a gang somewhere up country set to free him before you got him to the border. Way it looks to me."

Navarro considered. "About the way it's been looking to me, too. But we never heard of any outlaw gang linked up to Ferris. Anyhow, there're other possibilities. More I think of it. Well, there're a couple of girls in town, supposed to sing at the Laredo Lady. Cherry Gibbons and May Gibbons, sisters. Mosey around and manage to meet them. I don't think they would have anything to do with this. Just get a line on them, that's all." Navarro made a humorless grin. "Get word to Cherry, when you have a chance, that I'd be a good one for her to take up with. You know how to get that over. Tell her I'll be around."

"All right, Blackie. I'll take a look at the Gibbons pair."

"There's an old couple named Barton. Homesteaders, traveling in a wagon. See if—"

"They're camped in the wagon grove, over by Smith's Wagon Yard. Where all the broke nesters camp out. Saw 'em yesterday."

"How come?"

"Just happened to be over there. Smith mentioned them — said Barton was looking for a job, any kind of job, did I know of any —"

"Well, keep your eye on them. And there's one thing more, Gomez." He felt tenderly of his swollen eye. "A man named Dewey Lane. Rides a black horse, packs a Colt and Winchester carbine, young guy, dark, about my height but not as heavy, sort of educated — he may show up around here. Maybe at the hotel or some saloon. By God, that's an idea, maybe around those Gibbons girls. I want to know if he shows."

Gomez nodded. "You want him arrested?"

"Just let me know. We've got to watch our step — that damned Citizens Committee bunch is nosing around. When we take Lane we'll need an excuse that will stand up."

Navarro paced. "Gomez, how come that man Davis died on us?"

"*Dios!* That was bad. You did it too hard. Concussion. A bad accident."

"It wasn't an accident," Navarro said

thickly. "That was no ordinary drunk, that Davis. He'd been snooping around town for a week."

"How you mean, Blackie?"

"What I worked him over for," said Blackie slowly, "and what I never got him to say, was that I have a damned good hunch he was somebody paid to snoop around for the Citizens Committee."

Gomez whistled softly. He wore a worried frown when he went out. Navarro fingered his puffed eye and thought of the man who had given it to him. If the Gibbons girls hadn't been around — and that little bastard stage driver — he would have left Dewey Lane walking the rest of his life like Benecke. But it wasn't too late. Dewey Lane would be just the man to turn over to Sorro as the one who had liberated Rusty Ferris.

Dewey Lane's mind slowly emerged from a shroud of blackness. The deep throb of head pain subsided. He became aware of his surroundings, the hay smell heavy in Hagerman's barn, the cot beneath him, the blurred edge of a head bandage. Hagerman told him that he had been blacked out for two days. He filled the rest in, talking in his slow way, while Dewey drank the soup and coffee he had brought. The crossing,

Hagerman said, had gone down and all the others had pulled out forty-eight hours ago, Laredo bound.

"Navarro didn't stomp you. Benecke seen to that. The girls were watching by then, and I guess that stopped Navarro, too. He was beat up pretty bad. He was a little crazy after that boy got away from him. When the creek went down, he seemed glad to get out of here."

"He gave up trying to trace Rusty Ferris?"

"I reckon you've forgotten, all the stock was let out of the pen. By the time we rounded them up, it was too late. By then, Navarro was drunk anyhow, and mad to take it out on somebody, which was you. From tracks me and Benecke saw, Ferris was on a horse, in a high run west down the creek. I doubt they'll find that boy again."

By late afternoon, Dewey felt like walking about the station grounds. The place seemed strangely different. The group he had been thrown with for the brief, strained time when the creek had held them prisoners together, had vanished, gone their ways. The nesters' camp place in the mesquites was empty. The two bedroom doors inside the station hung open, the girls' luggage no longer in sight on the floor and Rusty Ferris's little cell lifeless except for a meandering hairy tarantula. Only the ashes of the Bartons' cook fire remained, smokeless now, and Lenman's fresh grave mound out east of the pen, and the beat-down earth and turf where he and Navarro had fought. After supper, Hagerman dressed his head again. He slept soundly through the night, and the next morning he told Hagerman that he felt able to ride.

Hagerman's big hands carefully took off the bandage. He seemed pleased with his doctoring. "Looks all right," he mumbled. "You're goin' to have a scar but your hair will cover most of it."

"You've done a good job with me, Hagerman."

The big caretaker retired into his own vacant distance. But Dewey thought Hagerman would talk more freely to him now. He asked, "You said something the other day, about the Temblers and the Laredo law, when I asked you about El Bar. What was it about them?"

"Around here, we always heard the Temblers was connected up to Sorro, across the border."

"That made trouble for El Bar?"

Hagerman nodded. "McCall was in the way. He told me once they brought the herds up the Road at night and crossed them over El Bar land, to get through to the Tembler place. That way they had the El Bar valley to go through, 'stead of coming over the bad roughs to the south. McCall was afraid. Finally, his hired hands got boogered and took out. The Temblers was makin' it rough, tryin' to run him off. Tried to burn his house. He bought supplies from me here at the station a few times, scared to go to town."

"Navarro?" Dewey prompted.

Hagerman nodded. "Sheriff Trevino — he's no more a sheriff than that tarantula in yonder — and Navarro, they run Laredo. Talk is, they stand in with Sorro across the border and the Temblers up here."

Dewey realized that El Bar obviously would be no picnic if he decided to stay. All along, he had carried the aimless feeling that he would probably just look at the place, for curiosity, and drift on, that the claim papers he carried had been only an excuse to ride somewhere. El Bar, as Hagerman pictured it, was no spot for a man singlehanded and without capital to build it up or to hire help, and bucking the combined forces that Hagerman pictured as running out McCall. Still his decision did not quite form itself. He would not hurry it.

When Dewey was ready to leave, Hagerman mumbled, "Good luck. If you need anything, this here's the nearest place." For Hagerman, it was an eloquent offer of friendship.

Riding toward the crossing, Dewey looked back and waved again to Hagerman, standing in the station doorway. He saw, in a moment's play of memory, Cherry and May as they had stood before Rusty's locked door that night, nervous and strained, under the deputies' heckling, singing of Chula Chalita and *mañana*. Well, *mañana* had come, all right, and Rusty Ferris with it. A cocked forty-five in his handcuffed fingers, and May's beautiful morning ready had unraveled fast.

He rode the black cautiously through the muddy drift left by the water, crossed the rocky bottom now running only flank deep, and pulled up on the Road on the south side. The big horse shook himself, and Dewey heeled him into a trot down the stage tracks. He sighted the rocky ledge of the landmark on his map, and pulled off the Road to the east. Somewhere ahead now, a few miles, he would strike the narrow valley, flanked on one side by the meandering Cibolo, and on the south by a jagged line of rocky low cliffs. From there on, if he read McCall's drawing right, he would be riding on his own grass. El Bar Ranch.

He recalled the Bartons' reaction to his mention of El Bar, almost as if the ranch name meant something personal to them. This made him consider, in turn, the hidden horse, the way Rusty had looked at the Barton camp, and then — had Cherry Gibbons deliberately moved into Navarro's path when the deputy had started for the door with gun raised, in pursuit of Rusty? Had May Gibbons been ignorant of drink mixing, or cleverly deliberate the night she had served Dewey's watered, the deputies' strong? Was she trying to put the lawmen in a stupor for the night?

Or were these things imagination? Had a pal of Rusty's maybe slipped in from the brush that night and pushed a gun into Rusty's hands through the window?

He wondered what would become of the Bartons, and their plodding journey from one bad time to another. And May Gibbons. Well, both the Gibbons girls. And the twisted hard-bitten Benecke, and old Hagerman. Even Rusty Ferris, on the loose somewhere with his gun and his manacled hands, unless his pals had freed him by now. Then a dull sense of loneliness closed down on him. It seemed crazy, but he had *liked* those people.

After a time he rode into a long valley,

stretching eastward between the naked cliffs on the south and the Cibolo on the north. He squinted in sudden interest.

The valley was thinly green with grass, better grass than he had ever expected to see in this country. Two leagues of it, or more, nearly fifteen sections, according to Mc-Call's papers. No wonder the Temblers wanted this land. As he rode, he strained with new interest to catch his first sight of the house that should lay somewhere ahead. The adobe house that McCall had said wasn't much, "But it'll keep the flies in and the coyotes out."

7

The El Bar burn showed dimly on the shaggy hindquarter of the first longhorn cow he sighted. Scrawny as the cow was, that El Bar was *his* mark. He tasted a peculiar sense of possession, of personal responsibility for this animal, her grass, water, and offspring. Awareness hit him that now he belonged to the select ranks of Texas men whose names, in effect, were engraved upon the land and the animals that grazed it. There was a vast difference in this, in seeing his identity linked with one half-wild longhorn cow, and his past impersonal trailing of thousands of them on far-off cattle trails with other men's brands of ownership making a hodgepodge of rump symbols under the indifferent eyes of hired riders.

In that moment, Dewey experienced a surge of attachment for the land, a near compulsion to put his hands to it and try to do something with it. He angled his course, riding for the half-hidden cuts and brush *motas* in hopes of seeing more El Bar stock. This meandering route flushed a fair-sized bunch of cattle, a hundred or more, where they watered at the shallow hole in the floor of a grassy arroyo. He turned across the flat, back toward the distant Cibolo treeline, in search of the house. Soon he sighted the scrawny grove of wind-blown cottonwoods, then the windmill tower and its unmoving blades, finally the squat dab of brown adobe that would be McCall's house. No, *his* house!

There was the house, beginning to show its scars, and a sagging porch awning; the stilled skeleton of the windmill and earthen water tank, a cedar-pole corral with gaps in the fence, a pole shed, knee-high broom-weeds all over the clearing. Neglect and deterioration were everywhere. He dismounted at the house. Its condition, on closer inspection, stirred him with an unusual hurt mixed with real anger against nobody in particular for the damage he saw. The porch awning was minus a corner log support and had dumped a portion of its brush and sod roofing to a musty pile upon the ground. The door swung open, hanging by one hinge. Where a part of the sod and brush roof had been pounded by weather, a gaping hole showed. A bracing of hewn logs which faced a portion of the adobe walls to give strength at each corner, showed peculiar black coloring. As he studied this, he saw that the logs at the near corner were charred nearly to cinders, and the fire stains streaked the mud brick wall extending to the rear corner. The fire had been set long ago.

Inside, the roof hole showed sky light. Dust and debris covered the wood floor and the few pieces of furniture. A disturbed dark shadow raised beady orbs of appraisal from the corner of the second room, then the small black snake made for an outside hole in the base of the back wall. Dewey took a second survey of the two rooms, and of the small kitchen leanto. He blew the white grit off the corner of a plank table, gingerly sat on the edge of it, and lofted a boot bottom to a pine bench. Something welled up inside of him that he turned into a hollow laugh, hurting his bruised ribs. *"Home!"*

During the remaining hours of daylight he rode the length of the valley, got the lay of his boundaries, and saw a few more El Bar cattle. At the far end of the grassy stretch he saw how the Cibolo cut across the meander southeast, toward the Rio Grande, thus effecting a natural boundary between El Bar and the Tembler land to the east. He could also see why his valley made a favorable cut-across from the Road to the Tembler land. If Sorro were delivering Mexican stock to the Temblers, as Hagerman had said, this was the easy way to get there. Up the Laredo Road, then eastward through El Bar, across the Cibolo, and onto Tembler range. Such a route evaded the long line of cliffs and rocky faults to the south.

Back at the cottonwood grove, just before dusk, he gave closer examination to the pole corral, and shed, and the windmill. All were rank with weeds. Poles were missing from the pen fence, leaving big gaps. The windmill gears, from the ground, looked rusted and locked, the pump rod jammed, the windmill tank and water troughs bone dry. What watering the cattle were getting had to be from the shallow water hole along the mid-valley cut.

Yet, he saw the possibilities here. The whole setup challenged him to roll up his sleeve, pitch in, and make something out of it. How to build up El Bar? He mused over that as he ate cold rations in the house at dusk. Knowing full well he was playing with an almost impossible idea, he let himself map a line of work he would pursue if he intended to stay.

First, he would clean and repair the

house. Replace the missing corral poles to make it horse-proof. Make a full tally of his cattle, see what he had in numbers. Put the windmill to working, to provide trough and tank water for the time when the arroyo hole would run dry later in the summer. He would have to obtain supplies — grub, tools, a dozen things. An understanding with the Temblers, if possible.

But he knew how much money he carried. A bare three hundred dollars. All he owned in the world, three hundred dollars to show for twenty-six years. Not enough to do the things that would have to be done. One man alone could not handle it, anyhow. Just the windmilling took two men, if rods had to be pulled. To say nothing of cutting poles on the creek for repairs, branding the calf crop, riding herd, flushing the strays out of the brush and cliffs and riding Tembler land for El Bar stuff that probably had strayed across the creek. Maybe bad trouble with the Temblers. No law to turn to for protecting his rights. How could he do it alone?

He stretched his bruised body for sleep, already trying to decide on which direction he would head tomorrow. *Mañana.*

Sleepily, he heard the night breeze outside the broken window whisper off-key, plaintive notes, thin and mighty lonesome. *Ma-*

ñana must be . . . say sí . . . say sí . . . See the sun stealing near, Chula Chalita . . . Might be he would ride to Laredo, Navarro or no Navarro, and see if he could borrow money on a mortgage of his cattle, enough to start operating. Might be he would see if Cherry Gibbons lived up to her looks. . . .

Next day, Dewey gave in to an impulse to ride the five-mile length of valley one more time for another look at near the south boundary line where the gullies led down to the Cibolo and sighted the two horsemen across on Tembler land.

They changed their course, after spotting him, and put their mounts scrambling across the creek, and up the rise. The man in the lead pulled up and said without preliminary, "I'm Jake Tembler. This is Frank Hanson, my foreman."

Tembler, a slender middle-aged man who sat his saddle with assurance and looked at Dewey the same way, packed a whole bundle of questions into his blunt introduction. He sucked in his colorless lips very tight, stretching the bleached line of a foppish mustache, waiting. Frank Hanson, a Mexican-dark hulk with a cloudy stare, brought his mustang around a little distance apart from Tembler, until Dewey had to turn from one to see the other.

"My name's Lane."

Tembler nodded. His nod took in the country around and back of Dewey. "When I see a rider on my land I haven't seen before, I like to know what he's doing and where he's going. I assume he ought to have a reason for being where he is."

"A fair assumption." Dewey matched Tembler's tight-lipped smile. "I didn't know this was your land."

"My place starts right there." Tembler lifted a thumb to the creek. "But I sort of look after this spread. For the owner. He's gone somewhere."

"He has?"

"Yeah." Tembler's expression turned stone cold. "I've asked you a question, Lane."

"I know you have. Just trying to figure how to answer it. I guess the answer is, the owner of El Bar has come back. Me."

Tembler nodded shortly, his gaze tight and shrewd, as if this were no surprise.

"You bought from McCall?"

"That's right."

"Got his papers and title, I guess. You aiming to run the place?"

Dewey hesitated. So far Tembler seemed mild enough, overlooking the blunt, cold way of getting to the point of things. Almost as if he could be friendly if he'd let himself.

Dewey remembered this hard caliber from past trails and places. They looked cold, frost-bitten even on a hot day, and they could keep looking that way when they gunned for your back.

"I haven't decided, Tembler." Curiously, he added, "You care to make an offer?"

"Yeah." Tembler shot a look to his foreman. Hanson cracked his face for a yellow-toothed grin. Tembler said, "I got a standing offer for El Bar. One hundred and ninety-nine dollars and two-bits."

Hanson made a belly-deep chuckle. "The two-bits is for the spread," Hansen added. "The hundred ninety-nine, that's charity for a neighbor. Jake, he's generous to a fault."

Tembler laughed. Dewey felt his face burning. Now he looked over the dapper Tembler and the ponderous foreman, giving his red flush of anger a second to cool. Hanson moved warily in the saddle with a cautious twist that brought his gun hip forward. Dewey thought bitterly, *They know they don't have to buy.*

He turned a narrow stare on Tembler, weighted with his dislike. Tembler studied the blood scabs and scars, the bruises made by Navarro's fists.

"I'll hear a serious offer," Dewey said.

"You heard one."

101

"Good God, Tembler! This is prize land. It joins right onto yours, it's worth something to you. What's wrong with talking sense?"

Tembler shot back, "It's just the way I decided to do business, Lane. McCall wouldn't take my offer, either — he lived to wish he had. Now I don't give a damn whether I buy it or not, at any price — I just decided on one hundred and ninety-nine dollars and twenty-five cents for the hell of it, and you can high-tail with that much or you can high-tail without it. I'll pick up the claim for nothing when you let it lapse."

"Then you're a fool, Tembler, for thinking I'm one. You come back with a grown-up man's proposition for this land. I might consider it. Might not."

Tembler whitened under his sunburn. He forefingered his fine line of mustache. Back of this annoyance Dewey saw all the power of the vast Tembler sections, stretching no telling how far east, with the weight of how many riders at his command, his lucrative stand-in with Sorro, north gateway for the flow of stolen Mexican cattle and horses. Tembler would not be crossed by anyone.

"Want to give him a little sample, Jake?" the foreman muttered.

"Don't draw it, Hanson," Dewey said.

"Why, you —"

"Keep still, Frank!" Tembler lifted his reins. "Lane, the day you take my offer might be the luckiest one you ever lived."

Dewey nodded curtly. "I'll think it over."

Hanson muttered, "Don't take too long to think. Jake might change his mind, most any time."

They whirled their horses and rode away in a dusty flurry, back across the slow-flowing Cibolo. Dewey knew Tembler would make him no fair offer, and evidently no other buyer was available in the whole region. Everybody would know about the Temblers. This border setup, he reflected, was a whole dynasty in itself, cut off from Texas law and order, running rampant down here with its powerful alliance of the Temblers, the Laredo law which was Navarro, and Sorro and his Mexican legion just across the border.

He wouldn't take Tembler's insane joke of an offer, he told himself. He would never give the man that much satisfaction.

That night he slept comfortably, with his muscle bruises now easing, as if this dilapidated little house had long been his home. Only once did he awaken, and that was with a quick-upright jump, hand going for his sixgun, at the sound of what he sleepily thought were footsteps in the yard. Listening tensely, he caught the faint shuffling noise again, and knew it had been no dream. Something, two-legged or four, was somewhere beyond the back corner.

He raised the Colt and moved across creaking boards to the open side window. Nothing was visible from there but the cottonwood shadows and black surf of blowing broomweeds. He moved to the back door and looked out, but the full darkness of the night closed off all things, even after he stood a long time to adjust his vision to it. Away off, he heard some moving sound. Finally he concluded that his visitor had been only a coyote, or perhaps a curious longhorn or antelope accustomed to the run of the yard.

When the gray dawn came he built a stove fire, cooked his breakfast, then went out to water his horse. When he saddled, he decided to ride on a swing across the back side of the grove to look for possible signs of last night's sounds.

He found no tracks that he could distinguish in the hard-packed earth and weeds. He moseyed his black on north, into a brushy section that sloped downward in a sweep toward the creek line. In a scatter of cedars and chaparral, he sighted a longhorn cow that backed off, pawing dirt as he approached. The horse stiffened its ears and flung its muzzle.

"Just a crazy cow," Dewey muttered. "You've seen 'em by the thousands."

The cow stopped, with its head peculiarly lowered, taking a nervous stance like a hound scenting plover. The horse shied and flung its bit.

Dewey had to tighten the reins and force the horse on toward the longhorn. The thick cedar clump he approached began to move in its lower branches. His first thought was the natural guess that a new-dropped calf was hidden in the cedars.

But this was a human form, and it came out of the brush tangle dead ahead. A dirt-streaked, deathly white face arose out of the earth, and tattered clothes and the blood-clotted dirty mess of a shoulder wound bandage. This thing unbuckled from the brush, a corpse with white eyes not yet quite dead. Two handcuffed wrists came up. The unsteady double set of fingers held a shaking sixgun with its muzzle limply waving at Dewey.

"Don't move," a voice said weakly.

"Good God — you're Rusty Ferris!"

Rusty's mouth worked futilely for sounds that wouldn't come, and then he tiredly began to kneel, dropping his hands, and the gun. He tumbled hard forward on his face and lay like a bundle of lost rags.

8

The first show of life from Rusty Ferris, other than his labored breathing, came half an hour after Dewey had unloaded the limp and dirty body from saddle to bunk in the dilapidated 'dobe.

He picked some of the blood-crusted rags off Rusty's shoulder wound, not sure whether he had opened a blood flow again, hurried out for wood and tried to get water boiling on the stove, kept coming back to the bed to see if Rusty was dead or still alive, and fiddled one idea after another as to what he should do.

He was standing over the pale, smelly thing stretched on his blanket, thinking that this would have called for a doctor, damned quick, and also the law, under any other circumstances. Somebody had to get that lead slug out of Rusty's shoulder if it was still beded inside the bluish flesh pulp. But the nearest somebody for that would be at Laredo, maybe four hours there and four back.

In some faraway borderland of death where he lingered, Rusty opened his eyes. He forced his parched lips to crack a little in a bid for the stranger's understanding of his only wish. As he lifted his locked hands a few inches off his chest. "Can you get these things off of me?" He closed his eyes and lowered his imprisoned hands. "I'm so tired of wearing them."

"We'll get them off. You take it easy now."

How in hell do you get handcufls off a wounded man?

"If I die, I don't want it to be in hand-cuffs."

"Well, now, you're not going to die."

"You're — Dewey Lane, wasn't it?" Rusty's eyes stayed closed.

"Yeah. Now I'm going to get you doc-tored. We're going to get that wound cleaned up."

He brought water, lifted Rusty as care-fully as he could with one arm circling the limp shoulder, and feel water to the fevered lips. The big job came next. He had to tear the last fragments of the matted bandage away. Some of the dead flesh and dried blood came with the cloth. After that, he found an old sliver of soap, made a pan of hot suds, and bathed the wound. Sometime during this process, Rusty passed out completely.

The wound didn't look quite as bad after the cleaning. A small blood flow started again, but Dewey grimly concluded he would have to risk even more blood loss. If the slug was in there, it had to come out. By now it was nearly midday. The air had turned hot. The dusty interior of the 'dobe took on heat, old flesh smells and the buzzing drone of invading green flies. Dewey took off his shirt, opened the long blade of his pocket knife and dropped the knife into the pan of boiling water. Now he had to go chop more wood, for the fire was dying. He did this at the meager mesquite woodpile, using McCall's rusted ax, hurrying it because what he had to do had to be done while Rusty was still unconscious. All the time the worry persisted that maybe he was too late. Maybe the bullet had started gangrene, and he was going to have to watch Rusty die by degrees, with his arm rotting off.

The surgical job was a messy one, and his body was running sweat before he had finished. He had seen it done once before, on an impassive Kiowa wounded by a herd rider on the Chisholm Trail. The crazy rider had come back later and killed the buck anyhow because the Kiowa had stolen his night horse. The slug was in there, all right.

Not deep, fortunately. The scalded knife point touched lead. Dewey clamped his teeth and pressed the blade down. and under, with more sweat bursting out on his face and Rusty trying to stir, moaning thinly.

Up came the ugly jagged wad of the thing, in a flow of fresh blood. Navarro's shot that had hit, or Lenman's carbine bullet he couldn't tell which. He felt weak enough for a moment to want to lie down beside Rusty, but the blood flow had to be stopped.

This he accomplished with a fresh bandage made from strips torn off the only clean garment in his saddlebag, a pair of thin ribbed drawers. He wished for medicine of some kind, any kind, for a disinfectant. He thought of all the emergency poultices he had ever heard of, glancing helplessly about the empty place. Nothing there he could put his hands on.

There was something else, though, probably just as important. Rusty had lost no telling how much blood. Dewey thought back — four days since he had been wounded, and no way of knowing whether he had eaten since. He had to get a little strength back into that wasted body or Rusty was done for. He dug into his grub bag and fashioned a soupy concoction of left-over frijoles, already once cooked, mixed with crumblings of sourdough bread and a little seasoning from salt bacon grease. It made a slow process, spooning this a little at a time into Rusty's limp mouth. He stayed with the task for an hour, it seemed to him until he had gotten a tin cup of the soup into Rusty's stomach. Then he wondered of he might be killing instead of curing the man. By then, it was time to whack some more dead mesquite limbs into stove-size chunks with the woodpile ax and start more water to boiling. The water had to be ridden for, at the cattle water hole. His horse had to be watered, too, and restaked in grass. He did these chores on the run, taking time to hurry over at intervals for a look at Rusty. With the second boiling of water he made coffee, found a small tied-rag of sugar in his grub bag, and again lifted Rusty and worked a few swallows of sugared coffee down his throat.

By late afternoon, Dewey felt whipped-down enough to have had a full day's hard range work behind him. Branding and cutting calves for a fourteen hour stretch had been a milder workout than this. He didn't know what he was going to do next about Rusty. What if he lived or what if he died? Somebody — some official somebody —

111

would have to know. Navarro's prisoner was one big unwanted problem either way.

It kept coming back, though, that the thing he had to do was save Rusty's life, if possible. "I've got no choice in that," Dewey told himself. "This must be the way a doctor feels. Even if the patient is going to hang as soon as he pulls him through."

He was standing in the doorway, sweaty, tired and baffled, when Rusty spoke behind him. Rusty's voice sounded so much stronger than his previous weak whispering that Dewey jumped.

"Lane . . . Dewey Lane. Where am I?"

"This is El Bar Ranch."

"El Bar. I saw your light . . . I must have been out a long time. My shoulder hurts like hell."

"I got the bullet out."

"Am I going to get to keep — is my arm all right?"

"Sure, it's going to be all right. What you need is some strength. Build some blood back in you."

Rusty searched up for a closer look. A whole cargo of questions had to be unloaded. Did he kill Lenman? Navarro? Were they riding on his trail now? Was Dewey Lane going to turn him back to the law? What had become of the others? The

Bartons? The girls? What made Dewey Lane's face look so beat up? And, once again, was he going to get those hated handcuffs off?

Dewey answered briefly, truthfully. In explaining his bruises, he had to say he had been in a fight with Navarro.

"Wonder he didn't stomp you. He will yet, if you cross him again."

"I might have something to say about that."

"If he comes this way looking for me, you're in trouble. Maybe by now he's looking for both of us."

Dewey expected that. Once Jake Tembler reported Dewey was at El Bar, as he was likely to do, Navarro would go on the warpath. It was just a matter of when Tembler called on his hired law. Any way he looked at it, Dewey thought, he was in for trouble with Navarro. And Rusty's showing up wasn't helping.

There must be a reason Rusty had headed for El Bar. A rendezvous here with somebody, believing the place was deserted?

"Feel like talking any more?"

"Naw." Rusty wearily closed his eyes. "I still don't know who you are. Don't pay to trust every stranger you meet."

"All right. Nobody's badgerin' you to talk."

Dewey worried about the wound. It was something a doctor ought to attend to. Did he dare leave the man alone for the time it would take to ride to Laredo and return?

The evening came on. Far off in the valley he saw the longhorns collect at the watering hole. Early dusk carried on the high strings of a breeze the vagrant tune-up howl of a coyote. He saw scuttling across the broom-weed-yard a disturbed civet cat, and heard, somewhere north, the lonesome whinny of a horse. Dewey stiffened to that sound. He brought his own horse up to the yard and saddled, then rode off in the gloom after taking a quick trip inside to look at the sleeping Rusty. He retraced his course to the cedars where Rusty had appeared, and soon found Rusty's horse. The mustang was still saddled and reined to a mesquite. It carried a blanket roll and a pair of saddlebags. He led the horse all the way to the water hole in the early darkness, waited until it drank its fill, which was a long time. He staked it for the night with his own, in the nearest grass, and lugged Rusty's blanket roll and bags to the house.

This was the horse he had seen tied out in the willows below the station. The hidden horse, sure as the world, that Barton had known about.

"In other words," Dewey mused, "this was the get-away horse and this saddle roll and these bags were no accident. And Rusty knew where to find them. And Barton knew I'd been down there."

Well, the sixgun hadn't crawled into Rusty's window that night all by itself, either. Barton, again? The way this now shaped in his mind, the whole setup at the station began to look a lot more prearranged than had met his eye before.

He slept fitfully, stretched on the cot beside Rusty's bunk. Several times he arose to bring water for Rusty, to see if his fever was diminishing, and once in the night he heard Rusty worriedly. *"Get these handcuffs off of me ... Lane ... I'm so tired of wearing 'em ..."* When he bent over Rusty, bathing his face and hot body with a wet rag, Rusty fitfully flung his manacled hands about. In the darkness, Dewey could see from memory those blood-streaked thin wrists, the worn cut places in the skin made by the handcuffs during Rusty's eternity of wearing them.

The sight of them in his mind was too much for Dewey. They had to come off. Maybe it was because just the sight of handcuffs revolted him. A man lost all his dignity when cuffs were snapped on. Himself a man who liked all the freedom there was to breathe and move in, in a big open country, and not even the authoritative touch of any other man's restraining hand upon him, he grimly imagined that handcuffs whittling on you was almost the second worst thing that could be done to a man. They turned him from an individual into an impotent chunk of meat, like a new-killed beef hoisted to a tree limb. Left him dangling dead inside, helpless all over, spirit included.

He tiptoed to the opening where the door swung on its one hinge and watched the half-curved body of a coyote drift sidewise into and out of the weedy shadows past the pole shed. Two chunky little tumbleweeds that were her pups loped hell-bent after the bitch. He breathed deeply of the night air, *his* night air, with its longhorn smell, and the waterhole, and April-new grass all blended within it. He tried to remember every item in his and Rusty's saddle bags, in the house, anywhere in the yard. What could a man find here that would cut through two brass bracelets? He got his final hour of delayed sleep on the cot with that concern his last conscious thought.

A voice spoke weakly, but clearly, beside him. "Lane — you awake yet? I sure could use a cup of coffee."

Dewey scrambled tall to his sock feet,

rummaged for matches and the drooped candle stuck in a tin can. Rusty showed a satisfying trace of his former good color. His eyes smiled in the flickering light, and he even managed to grin.

Dewey grinned back, pleased. The canteen and bucket rattled dry. He would have to ride for the water hole. And a few dead mesquite sticks, while he was at it.

"Sure, we got coffee, Rusty. I'll be back in a minute." He strapped on his gunbelt. "Don't you go off."

Rusty chuckled, coughed, then groaned. "*Sí* I'll stay right here. You got my shoulder nailed to the bunk, anyhow, feels like. What did you use, a railroad spike?"

"Had to," Dewey retorted. "You're a hard hombre to hold in one place."

He was back in a short time with an awkward burden of canteen and a blanket trundle of mesquite sticks. In a little while, the 'dobe's chimney belched its gray tassel to the pink morning. Coffee was boiling, the sourdough was warming, and salt bacon frying. Rusty woke up from another hard sleep.

"You going to be all day with that coffee?"

"When they start bitchin' about grub, they're getting well. You'd better eat hearty, mister. After breakfast, we've got another operation to do."

"Not poking in my shoulder again with that knife!"

"This operation's apt to be worse. We're going after that brass jewelry on your wrists. That is, if I can find something to work with and if you've got the strength to sweat out the job."

Rusty's glance hunted over the room. "My jacket," he murmured. "It's somewhere. Look in the side pocket."

"For what?"

"There's a chisel in it."

Dewey stared down at Rusty. "You think of everything, don't you? Where, out there in the brush, did you happen to run across a cedar tree growing a chisel?"

Rusty took the cup down to grin warily. "It came with the sixgun," he said.

9

Dewey went to the woodpile and brought back the ax. "Got to find another piece of steel, something to brace the cuffs while I hammer. You didn't by chance get an anvil with the gun and chisel, did you?"

When Rusty weakly shook his head, Dewey demanded, "Who was going to wield the chisel, anyhow? How the hell did somebody think you were going to use it? With your teeth? You wouldn't have a sidekick out somewhere, supposed to meet you, would you?"

Rusty opened his eyes and gave him a hard look. "You going to make palaver all day or get to work on these things?"

"I'm going to cut off your hands," Dewey retorted. "Easiest way to slip off the cuffs. Tell me, before you took to murdering Mexicans, did you ever know a nester family named *Barton?*"

Rusty's gaze moved about the sagging sod ceiling. "You got a nice place, Lane."

"I like it. With the windows out, you get so many unexpected varmints dropping in on you. Not all of them four-legged."

Finally, Dewey used an iron stove lid as a support for Rusty's hands. He turned Rusty sideways on the bunk, fitted the cuffs down to the lid, and started to work with the chisel and the ax head. It was slow and tedious, as he knew it would be. Rusty at intervals was forced to ask for relief from his shoulder pain in that position. Slowly the hammering went on as the day wore along. At last the chisel bit through the battered lock of one cuff and Dewey grunted with satisfaction. The manacle could be pried open later. He started on the other wrist.

His own fingers were cut, and Rusty's wrists were oozing blood from their old scars, when the fetters finally came off. Dewey tossed the ax, chisel and broken cuffs to the floor and stood, fagged out from his exertions. Rusty waited a moment, as if unsure he could part his hands. Childishly awed, almost, and with an expression that Dewey had never seen on a man before, Rusty raised his hands. He spread them slowly apart, as if showing the size of a fish, and he kept doing this, back and forth. A slow, sunrise kind of pleased wonderment came over him.

When Rusty spoke, it was in a tone of forced lightness, is if he strained to keep this an ordinary thing. He called, "You know, Lane, I'm going to remember you in my will. In case I ever make a fortune."

"Don't worry," Dewey grunted. "You'll make one all right."

After a silence, Rusty spoke again, with casualness. "Funny country, Texas, isn't it? You meet strange people, from everywhere. I think, Lane, that under some other conditions, somewhere 'way back, you and I would have been friends, if we'd run across one another."

Dewey shrugged. He might have admitted a like feeling, but the big truth was written out there across the whole hot prairie that now that he had this man out of handcuffs, his own predicament was by no means settled. What did he do with Rusty Ferris now? He was practically out of food, for one thing. His own meager supply, brought from Hagerman's place, and the few provisions he found in Rusty's bag, wouldn't last forever. There was no way of knowing whether Rusty's shoulder wound had a serious infection that could spread — only sane thing was to find a doctor somehow. Rusty couldn't stay on a horse. Even if he could, how would he look leading Rusty, limp and weak as a rattler-bit sheep, down the main street of Laredo inquiring for a doctor, and with Deputy Sheriff Navarro maybe the first to get word of their arrival? For that matter, where did it leave *him,* helping a killer who was already under an extradition order to Mexico signed by the Governor of Texas?

When he turned around to Rusty's bed, his anger at the whole problem, the unfairness of it, evidently was plain. Rusty, in his fevered lightheadedness, must have decided to ride over it with banter. "Your squaw must have been gone tribe-hopping for quite a spell. Your place looks way behind in its housekeeping."

"Listen, Ferris!" Dewey towered viciously over him. "Now you listen hard. I cut the lead out of you, and I toted and carried for you in a way one man damned well don't relish doing for another man, and I busted off the handcuffs that were feverin' you so bad. Now as that, I'd have done the same for a pair of lobos, or shot 'em, and for that you don't owe me a Chihuahua centavo. But there're two sides to this deal. As far as I'm concerned, until you make it different, the law wants you for murder. Some court in Coahuila says you're their boy, legal, signed, sealed, and still undelivered. I can't make you vanish, Ferris — much as I'd like to.

122

You're here on my hands. I can't ride off like you didn't exist, and I can't settle down here for life and raise you like a maverick calf. Now —"

He saw the feverish burn in Rusty's eyes. "Don't you think I know it? You've saved my life — up to now, anyhow. Not too sure about my arm, but anyhow, I'm alive, and that's thanks to you. What should I do? You ask me."

"I'm not asking you one damn thing!" Dewey snapped. "I'm not badgering a man hurt as bad as you are for a lot of answers — you just decide on your tune, and play it."

Rusty narrowed his gaze. "You think I'm a bad one? An outlaw?"

"How the hell would I know what you are?"

"I killed a man in Mexico Where does that leave us?"

"Just fine, Rusty. Just damned fine — all safe and cozy here. Navarro, the Governor of Texas, the State of Coahuila — they won't mind a bit if I help you skip the hanging."

"Don't ride me, Lane. Trouble with a thing like this, nobody believes me. Not a sonofabitch one of 'em would listen — the Angelo marshal, the judge up there, nobody. They turned me over to Navarro, like a little railroadin' of a man to a Mexican firing squad was nothing, nothing at all. I got cured of trying to make somebody listen."

"I'm listening."

"But you see, don't you, why I haven't thought it would be any use? Hell I didn't *know you*. You're just somebody who came along at a good time, saved my life. But I haven't had the breath to waste to see if you would believe me. The truth is" — Rusty's labored words faded away to a helpless mumble — "I've been scheming how I could get a gun on you, after I had the strength, and ride out of here. It's no use . . . I can't ever make it." Then, from far off, "Gun wouldn't have done it, anyhow. I couldn't throw a gun . . . on . . . you. . . ."

Dewey drifted to the doorway, letting Rusty rest a little. Toward the Cibolo tree line, he saw a small rise of dust. After a time, he made out the small dots of three riders, coming west up the valley. In another few minutes, these took shape as they headed toward the house. Dewey examined his sixgun. He searched worriedly for sight of his and Rusty's horses, staked to graze a distance north of the yard, and was thankful that intervening brush cut off sight of the two animals. He returned the ax to the woodpile and hid the battered pieces of the handcuffs under the wood.

He kept just within the shadows of the doorway, watching. And then, as he moodily debated on the best way to handle whatever was coming, Rusty stirred himself and decided to talk.

"That extradition business . . . you listening to me, Lane? There was no extradition. The Governor of Texas never heard of me. Navarro signed those papers, *himself*. Forged the whole business."

"Why would he do that?"

"They wouldn't believe me, up at Angelo. You don't believe me, either. The Angelo marshal turned me right over to Navarro and Lenman. I'd been on the run only two weeks, how did they think Navarro could go to Austin in that time, get an extradition hearing, come back and ride all the way up to Angelo and get me? He and Lenman, they were out for the money. Sorro was paying them a thousand dollars to get me across the border. Something else — Navarro knows that I know about the Sorro bunch, and his stand-in with them on this border business. He thought he couldn't afford to have me on the loose."

The horsemen were in plain sight now. They kept coming, their horses at a slow trot, headed for the adobe. Dewey began to recognize the silhouette of the center rider — Jake Tembler. One of the other was his foreman. "Go ahead, Rusty."

"It's such a damned long story," Rusty said wearily. "I was riding for Sorro — it was a job for me, when I started, and I didn't know what I was getting into. We — I — needed money. You know how it's been all over Texas. A man would take any job. Anyhow — we had this trouble. At a fiesta, one night. The bunch was drunk, and that was an ugly bunch. There was a señorita. She made too much of a play for me, and Little Mike — that's Sorro's son — or was — he got murdering mad over it. The upshot — he came at me with a knife. This was no playin', and next I knew he was doing his best to kill me, and I was hemmed in, couldn't run, and Little Mike said, 'Watch me cut the gringo's throat!' Lane — I never before pulled a trigger on a man in my life. But I grabbed a gun off the nearest man, and just as Little Mike came in with that long blade, I plain shot my way out of there. I shot Sorro's boy, killed him, and got out of there on the blackest night you ever saw and started running. Two nights later I swam the Rio Grande, and I didn't have a nickel, or know a human down here, so I stole a horse and kept going. They got me at Angelo. By then the word was out everywhere. Sorro and Navarro saw to that. So one fine day, there in the Angelo calaboose, here came Navarro and Lenman, the big law men from Laredo, having good-time drinks with the Angelo marshal and showing the extradition papers for Rusty Ferris."

Dewey believed him. This was no border scum. Rusty was an educated man, and now that Dewey knew Navarro, as well as Rusty, he could visualize the plot, the prisoner's run of hard luck and trouble. There were still gaps. Who had trailed Rusty on Laredo Road, engineered the escape plot, the smuggled gun? Barton? One thing he knew — he had to help Rusty complete his escape. He'd never let the Laredo law lay hands on him again if he could prevent it.

"Rusty, company's coming. Jake Tembler and Frank Hanson, his foreman. And a third man."

A low whistle sounded from the bunk. "I know Jake Tembler. Saw him, at least, one time at Sorro's place. Can they see my horse?"

"Both horses are out of sight. They won't see them unless they ride north of the house."

Dewey put his Winchester within reach of Rusty. "I don't know what this is going to turn in to. Tembler wants to make sure that I'm leaving, I imagine. You keep quiet and don't stir, unless there's trouble."

As the riders halted in the yard, he walked to the edge of the bedded-log porch with its sagging roof corner. The three men were armed with leg Colts, and Tembler also carried a saddle carbine. The foreman, Frank Hanson, looked the most wrought-up of the trio, but there was no compromise in Tembler's expression.

"I see you haven't pulled out yet, Lane. We don't like it crowded on this range."

"You're the big auger that's doing the crowding. You ever hear the news that this is a free country?"

"You'd do well to take my offer, Lane. The offer don't stand past right now. You just hand me your papers and I'll hand you one hundred and ninety-nine dollars and twenty-five cents."

Dewey doubted if Tembler was much for stringing out conversation — looked as if all three had made the ride for some purpose stronger than talk. Main thing was to get rid of them before they decided to take a look inside.

"I'll think it over, Tembler."

"Thinkin' time's over."

"What's the rush?"

Hanson held his droopy stare on Dewey, saying, "I doubt if his papers are legal, noways, Jake. Maybe we ought to turn him over to the law."

"Yeah. Maybe this is a gent for Navarro to handle," Tembler smiled.

The third rider, when Hanson muttered. *"Rollins!"* nudged his horse, changing his location to a small distance from the others.

Dewey demanded, "What makes you so dead-set against having neighbors, Tembler?"

"I have my own reasons. Takes a big range for my operations, and I don't like being crowded by little two-bit spreads." He nodded contemptuously to indicate the adobe. "Your house is falling in, windmill's broke, corral full of holes — hell, you ain't *got* a place. Not even worth what I'm offering — I just plain want to get shed of you. Why, I'm being generous."

Hanson chuckled. Tembler slapped his hand on his gun holster in a movement of finality and snapped, "Take it or leave it!"

Dewey said, "I'll leave it."

It was on Dewey's lips to add that he would consider a sensible offer. A peculiar movement by the third rider, Rollins, a sun-blackened beanpole with a cushion of chin whiskers, stayed him. Rollins chose that moment to raise his hand and shade his eyes as if just sighting something at the top of the porch corner.

"Whole place fallin' in, like Jake says!" Rollins declared with mock astonishment. He took up his rope and shook out a loop. "Jake, what'd you say we make this porch corner look the same as the other'n, 'fore it falls and hurts somebody?"

This threat clamped Dewcy's jaws into hard knots. Tembler, watching him, could read the sudden surge of stubborness and anger. "Might be a good idea, Rollins."

With dull hatred for these men, for the uselessness and stupidity of what Tembler must have told Rollins to do, Dewey narrowly watched Rollins make a quick upwind throw of the loop that caught the protruding end of the peeled corner post. Rollins took a couple of quick turns of the lariat around his saddle horn.

"Might as well be all the way down as half," Hanson said. "Pull 'er. Rollins."

Rollins spurred his horse sideways, and the rope stretched taut. "Better move, feller — gonna be a mess of sod and brush comin' down!"

Tembler laughed "It ought to make a good bonfire, if you accidentally set it."

"Don't pull that post out!" Impulse shot

Dewey forward in angry strides toward Rollins. The rider coaxed his horse, grinning now and making the post sway from the rope strain.

"Stay where you are, Lane," Tembler called. Dewey saw the Colt revolver hanging in Tembler's hand. "You stand right there."

Hanson grunted, "Put some pull on it, Rollins."

Rollins threw his head back and gave a wild, "Yip-peeeeeeee!" socking in his spurs at the same time. His mustang sprang in a side leap. The porch post shot out, and the entire strip of narrow porch roofing came crashing down. Dust from sod and rotted poles enveloped the whole front of the house. With one look at the wreckage, Dewey felt his blind-red anger turn into something cold as a norther in his veins, steadying him all over.

"You made a mistake, Tembler."

Before Tembler could bring his arm up, Dewey ducked under the neck of Rollins's horse, flung himself hard again Rollins's left leg and saddle skirt, and savagely sank his fingers into Rollins's belted waist. In the same flow of muscle power he dragged Rollins bodily out of the saddle, with the horse plunging and Rollins clawing at rope and saddle horn. Rollins came loose in a

131

slanting, unbalanced dive and Dewey hit him at the point of his black whiskered chin as it went past. Bone cracked bone, and Rollins lay in the dirt where he fell. The horse side-stepped away in fright, still anchored by rope and pole, and with this movement Dewey lost a shield between himself and Tembler and Hanson. Before he could recover his own balance, the spat of a Winchester carbine streaked fire from a window.

Tembler's raised sixgun flew out of his hand. With an oath of pain, he jerked his head for a look toward the house, and Hanson with him. Dewey saw the slim muzzle of the Winchester resting on the window edge, trickling smoke, with the dim outlines of a man's head bent to the gun stock in the gloom behind it.

"You can drop your gun on the ground, too, Hanson," Rusty called.

Dewey had his own gun fisted. "Turn it loose, Hanson."

The foreman gingerly pulled his gun and dropped it. Dewey stooped and dragged Rollins's gun from its holster.

"Tembler, you and Hanson get down."

Tembler, white-faced, slowly got out of his saddle. He muttered angrily to Hanson. The foreman reluctantly dismounted.

Dewey motioned with his Colt. "Stand aside from your horses. In the house, there — keep the rifle on them a minute."

"It's on 'em," Rusty retorted.

Dewey gathered in the reins of the three horses. released Rollins's rope, and led the animals over to the pen gate, where he tied them up. When he came back, Tembler and Hanson stood as he had left them. Rollins sat up and felt of his chin. With his left hand, the gun ready in his right Dewey picked up the ax and tossed it at Tembler's feet.

"That stand of pinoak saplings yonder. Go cut two straight ones, the same size as these porch poles. I want 'em trimmed."

"I'm cutting no — !"

Dewey's right hand flicked. The three men facing him jumped from the sixgun's roar as loose dirt spewed across Tembler's boot.

"The next one will take off some toes, Tembler."

Tembler picked up the ax. He turned and trudged toward the sapling stand, fifty yards out. "They're not big enough to hide in, Tembler," Dewey called. "This Winchester's going to be drilled on your backbone all the time."

Hanson warily licked his lips. Sweat rolled down his chin. "You must be tired of livin'."

"I got a job for you, too, Hanson." Dewey went over and nudged Rollins with his boot. "On your feet."

Groggily, the man managed to stand erect, his glazed eyes holding to Dewey's cocked gun.

"You help Hanson. The two of you start clearing the rubbish out of the way."

Like a stunned bull, Hanson twisted his head from the sixgun drilled on him, to the Winchester barrel poking from the window. He plodded over and clumsily started tearing into the tangled mess of the collapsed awning. Rollins pitched in more readily. From the pinoak stand, the sound of Tembler's ax strokes began. As if to remind him that he was under close scrutiny, Rusty put a Winchester slug whining down that way to splash bark off the tree just above Tembler's hat.

Dewey stood a little way out in the yard, watching Hanson and Rollins, with a frequent glance down at Tembler.

After a time, his heart pounded and then seemed to stop beating. But they had not seen what he had seen. With forced casualness. he edged past Hanson and Rollins, stepped through the partly cleared space before the door, and lounged against the facing.

"Don't slow up," he told them. "First man that raises his head gets blown all the way back to Tembler land."

With that, he ducked inside. Without holstering his gun, he scooped Rusty up from the floor like lifting a baby calf, deposited him on the bed in three fast strides. He snatched the Winchester carbine from where it had fallen. He was back lounging in the door in no more than a fast count of ten for the whole operation. He walked to the yard with the carbine cradled, so that Tembler could see it if he looked that way.

"When your boss brings those two corner posts," Dewey said, "we'll build a new porch roof."

After a time, he sent Rollins down to help Tembler carry the peeled logs. Tembler came unsteadily, sweating and weak. Dewey backed off, switched the rifle to his left hand, drew his sixgun. He was thankful that the bed and Rusty's passed-out form, down the wall in the lefthand corner, would be out of their vision from doorway or window.

The job required three hours. In that time, the Tembler men never speaking, set the corner poles, raised the salvaged supporting logs for rafters, covered the top with brush, cut clumps of grass sod and tamped them into place. By then it was nearly sundown.

"How far to your headquarters from here, Tembler?"

Tembler gave him a haggard look. He was covered with dust and grimy sweat. "Twelve miles."

"You can make it 'way before midnight. Start walking."

"What!"

"I'll turn your horses loose tomorrow. Don't try to come back for 'em nor for any other purpose. Anything seen moving out here tonight will get shot at."

Tembler and his two riders turned together for incredulous looks into the long stretch of distance eastward. For a moment, Dewey thought sure they were going to jump him, gun or no gun. He tightened his finger on the trigger. Their hate came off their bodies like a sweat stink, and Tembler visibly shook. He strained for what little dignity he could salvage out of his humiliation. "Lane, not a man in the world can do this to me and live to tell it."

"Get moving, Tembler."

Tembler turned and started walking and he did not look back. Grunting curses, Hanson walked after him and then Rollins. Dewey watched a long time, until they plodded as three slow-moving dots, strung out, far off in the vally dusk.

So there went Tembler. How long until Navarro came riding?

He went inside and put down the Winchester, brought water and a rag, began to bathe Rusty's face that felt fevered again. He had only a numb, almost indifferent knowledge that he had burned all bridges now, that it was run or fight the Temblers and Blackie Navarro. Rusty at last stirred, and tried to sit up.

"You fainted on me," Dewey commented. "And when I saw that, *I* damn near fainted. The strain was a little too much for you."

"Damnedest thing I ever saw in my life," Rusty breathed. "Did they get the porch fixed back?"

"They did. Thanks for showing up with the Winchester when you did."

Rusty lay back, but he strained to see Dewey's features in the dim light. A taut grin touched Rusty's mouth. "Lane," he murmured, "I like the way you do business."

10

Dewey brought their two horses up and saddled them, telling Rusty that they were heading for the stage station. "I've got to cache you somewhere while I go to La- redo."

"Damn it! I've had enough of that place to last a lifetime."

"You hold on to the horn and save your breath."

When the starlight showed him that Rusty was weaving, he made a halt for rest and stretched Rusty in the grass. Rusty showed fevered uneasiness. "I don't like going back to the station, Lane. What's the idea?"

"You rather have Hagerman looking after you while I go for a doctor, or the Tembler bunch?"

"I'd rather stay hid out around the shack."

"Why?" Dewey demanded. "What's the big attraction for El Bar?"

"The scenery."

"The scenery and the chisel in your pocket. Seems to me you were hellbent to

138

get to El Bar." He propped on his elbow and peered at the dark form. "Who was to meet you there? You had it all arranged, didn't you? Who was due to come along and cut those handcuffs off you? Barton?"

"Nobody! I was taking my own chances."

"Liar."

Rusty shifted, grunting with the pain of the movement. "You giving up that El Bar place? I'd partner you with it, Lane, if I had this trouble lifted off me. It's got possibilities. You've got grass. Patch up that house, fix your windmill, sell off some cows to buy some saddle stock. Then we'd start branding all the mavericks running wild over west of here. There're thousands of 'em, wild as buffalo, nobody's brand on them. We could build a ranch out of this, a real outfit. Just one thing it needs."

"I can think of twenty. What was the particular one *you* thought up?"

"That house — it needs a woman's touch."

"Sure. That would solve everything."

"Woman makes a lot of difference."

"I'd be agreeable to trading you for a Tonkawa squaw. Or maybe to Sorro for a good-looking Mexican *puta*."

"He would be glad to trade." Rusty gave a weak laugh. "Damn you, I was talking seriously."

Dewey chuckled. "All right. I can think of a woman I wouldn't mind having here. And not for just housekeeping. Did you get a good look at that Cherry Gibbons? Now she's one I wouldn't mind sharing the luxuries of El Bar with for a spell —"

He saw Rusty's squirm. But nothing else he said brought so much as a mumble out of Rusty. Dewey sensed that a crazy strain had come between them in the darkness. He said stiffly, "We've got to be riding. Hagerman took pretty good care of me. I think he might do the same for you while I go to Laredo."

Sometime before midnight he aroused Hagerman at the station. The gaunt keeper listened blankly to Dewey's explanation and request, then agreed quickly, adding, "I don't like Navarro." They bedded Rusty at the barn in a gear room. "You fetch Doc Orr," advised Hagerman after looking at Rusty's wound. "He's one man in Laredo you can trust."

Rusty had a feverish request to make. "Tell those nesters. You tell them about me, Lane. . . . You do that. . . . They would want to know. . . ."

Outside, Dewey asked Hagerman, "You know anything about those Bartons?"

"Never saw 'em before. You goin' to have

trouble if you run into Navarro."

"If I don't come back within a day after the doctor has been here, will you move Rusty back to El Bar in a wagon?"

"What for?"

"I think someone meant to meet him there. Take him back after he's doctored and keep your wagon and yourselves hidden in the brush close to the shack. I'll come back there and take him off your hands. If I don't, somebody else may show up. I feel sure of that."

Hagerman mumbled, "I'd like to know who you think's comin' to find him at El Bar."

Dewey grinned to himself. "I couldn't tell you in a thousand years, Hagerman, why I'm letting this boy be as much trouble to me as he is. Maybe it's because I want him to get well. So he can help me start up El Bar again."

"That's a crazy notion."

"It damn sure is."

Dewey walked to his horse. Hagerman, following, had a worry of his own to relate. "Got the news yesterday the stage company's gone broke. They're closing down the line to Angelo. Been expectin' it. Before long, I got to go to town and look for a job."

Dewey said, "Too bad," and rode away.

There's just so much a man can worry about.

He forced the unwilling black over the crossing, and south on Laredo Road. This was the craziest night ride a man ever started, he thought. And yet how could he do otherwise? Riding to Laredo for a doctor for a wounded fugitive he barely knew. Riding, too, for another purpose — his now fully formed intention to hunt money or credit enough to hold on to El Bar. All of this among strangers, in Navarro's town.

He asked himself, half angrily, was he just damn-fool set on exposing himself to a fight with Navarro? He felt he had a settlement to collect from the deputy, for both himself and Rusty. But was it worth gambling his hide to go full-tilt into trouble he might avoid? Avoid how? By streaking out of here like a spotted ape. Now, Tonight. And to hell with Rusty, Navarro, the Temblers. . . .

No. He wanted El Bar. Bad enough to make this ride. That, and the need to get a doctor for Rusty. He kept riding south.

He came in sight of the awakening town with the sun, soon sighted a livery stable sign, and left his horse there. He walked sleepily down the deserted street and came to the hotel which was not yet astir. Just as he reached the entrance, he caught sound of a galloping horse coming that way on the side street. He turned and saw the rider. Even at a distance, in the dawn light, the set and size of the man looked familiar. Navarro.

Dewey stepped backward into the hotel doorway. The deputy swung his horse at the opposite corner, coming into the main street. It appeared that Navarro looked full at him, even as he stepped behind the screened doors. But the deputy did not slow. He passed so close that Dewey saw the drawn lines of Navarro's concentration. Then dust moved between them. Navarro rode north, up Laredo Road. Dewey emerged to the walk, watching Navarro until he was lost in the distance.

The clerk eyed him curiously as Dewey came in again and went across to the desk and registered. As Dewey climbed the stairs to his room, he wondered if Navarro had been summoned by Tembler, if he now rode for El Bar. Whatever his mission was, it would suit him just as well if it kept Navarro out of town all day.

He slept until noon. He cleaned up, put on a change of clothes from his war bag. For a little while he watched from his window the foot, burro and saddlehorse movement in Hidalgo Street. Two streets to the west he saw the barred windows that proclaimed Navarro's jail. Down the main street toward the river he saw the shouting sign of the Laredo Lady. It was painted the full length of the building above a row of narrow second-floor windows. He visualized the Gibbons sisters, backed nearly against Rusty's locked door, singing their *mañana* song, with Lenman drooling and Navarro's mind obviously making his own *mañana* plans for Cherry.

He knew the uneasy qualms of a chance meeting with Navarro, or running into Jake Tembler or his foreman. Still, a man had to have free movement. The force of a decision already formed hit him with great finality. It had been there all the time, inevitable, through his days of riding south with a deed and a map in his pocket. He had come to El Bar to build a ranch, had come to stay.

Now he buckled on his gunbelt with unhurried deliberation. With his purpose settled in his own mind, all the loose ends of his intentions seemed to clear like lifting fog in a valley, making his needs and his work begin to stand clear. One of the first jobs was to find out for certain whether Rusty Ferris had told the truth. Befriending a man being railroaded was one thing, but befriending a criminal was another. A lot depended on that. And he thought he knew how he could prove what he believed: that Rusty had told the truth. He found writing material, printed out a message and signed it. *Please find if Governor issued extradition Mexico one Rusty Ferris. Reply quickly care Laredo stage agent.* On the face of the envelope he wrote: *Dan Blocker, Editor, Austin Statesman, Austin, Texas,* and sealed the message inside.

At 1:15 the daily stage of the San Antonio line came shagging in from Beeville, the first railhead northeast. At 1:30, the station agent looked up and saw Editor Ed Carlos at the counter. The agent shook his head. "Nothing for you, Mr. Carlos."

At 1:45 Carlos entered the back office of the Texas Hardware Store. Peyton Evans, the store owner, looked up inquiringly. Carlos shook his head. "Nothing from Ranger headquarters yet. I can't understand it. Reckon they're just not going to pay any attention to us?"

"I've spotted the deputy, Gomez, going in and out of there," Evans said. "You suppose Navarro is having messages checked?"

"Not sure about anybody," Carlos said grimly. "This is a sick town. If our bunch can work up a case here on the quiet, maybe we can get the Governor to pay some attention to our troubles."

"But Godamighty, look what happened to Davis!"

"I know," the editor said bitterly. "Navarro pistol-whipped him to death. I think it's time we got our committee together and took things in our own hands. If things are ever going to be cleaned up in this town we've got to do it with our own guns."

They talked of this a while, then Peyton Evans changed the subject. "Did you ever know a newspaper publisher named Lane, up in the Panhandle?"

"Sure did. We learned the printing trade together in Fort Worth years ago. He had a paper in Caprock. Died a while back, I heard."

"His son was in here while ago. Dewey Lane." Evans thoughtfully lit a cigar. "He's traded for El Bar."

"Jake Tembler and Navarro won't let him stay long," Carlos predicted. "They ran McCall off."

"He needs finances," Evans said slowly. "Wanted credit for supplies. I stalled, but I'd like to see him raise a grubstake so he could operate the place. Have the notion he wants to tackle it and is a man that could do it."

"Where'd he go? I'd like to meet any son of Jesse Lane's."

"Said he was trying to find Doc Orr. He headed for the Laredo Lady."

"You keep a tight jaw on this other business till we can call a meeting," Carlos said before departing. "I think time's near for us to hit. We need to catch those outlaws red-handed in a big deal, like delivery of that horse herd being collected across the river. If we can just spring the trap on that one . . ."

"Our bunch has got their guns cocked and are ready to hit when we give the word," said Evans. "We've got three kingpins to worry about, as I see it. Sorro, Navarro and Tembler. If we can get the goods on them, their whole operation ought to fall apart. Then this town could quit hurtin'."

At 1:50, Deputy Sheriff Gomez stood on the walk in front of the stage station to take mental stock of Navarro's instructions to him for checking up on those people who had been in the stage station the other night. He had pretty well followed them out, he thought. The nester Barton and his wife were still camped at the wagon yard, with Barton going around hunting a day-labor job. The Gibbons sisters were singing at the Laredo Lady. He had met them and suggested to Cherry that Navarro would be a useful friend to have in this town. And he'd told May, the younger sister, that he, Gomez himself, wouldn't be a bad sort to cotton to either. Navarro had ridden north on receipt of an urgent order from Jake Tembler. Ought to be back by late afternoon.

Gomez, with it all checked off, now sauntered down the plank walk toward the Laredo Lady with a beer in mind before a siesta in the jail. Inside he spotted the man, editor of the *Laredo Sentinel*, standing at the far end of the bar. Carlos was talking with a tall stranger who had a hard, prairie look to him, and a hard, worn Colt sagging his old leather holster. The stranger's features came to Gomez's notice. The man obviously was bruised up, a crusty blood stripe down the front of his ear, like a mean bronc had thrown him in rocks. Not as beat-up as Navarro had looked, though.

Gomez asked the barkeep, "The canary birds up and around yet, Ponch?"

"Still sleepin'."

Gomez squinted up at the dark balcony. "Tell them I was inquirin' about them. I'll be back."

"*Sí*. Cherry will be glad to know you ain't forgot her, I doubt if she slept a wink, worryin' about you."

Gomez headed next for the hotel to make his daily checkup on who had registered in since yesterday. Navarro and Tembler had been mighty concerned in recent weeks about any strangers, and where they came from.

Cherry Gibbons sat before the peeled mirror in her bedroom on the second floor of the Laredo Lady, brushing her hair with rapid strokes. The mirror gave back a troubled face, still showing sleep traces. May Gibbons, murmuring a drowsy, "Good morning," came in from the adjoining room. Makeup and stage costumes provided no disguises now. They looked like what they were, two fagged-out night-time performers struggling to come alive for a new day, the cheek rouge off and the guard of make-believe down. Last night had been another big one in the Laredo Lady. The Gibbons Sisters, in their midnight singing act, had tossed their curls and smiled their wide painted smiles, and had striven for harmony before the wasp nest of eyes and open mouths out in the fog of smoke, tequila sweat and male hunger.

Across at the wall in Cherry's cubbyhole of a room, stood a low single-width iron bed, its sheet and quilt tangled, and this was matched by an identical one visible through the door to May's room. The Laredo Lady put up its performers on its rambling second-floor hive where a girl could unlock her door in the small hours according to individual and independent arrangements premade. The walls and twisting balcony corridor leaked even the tiniest noises, and just one taxed cot spring was apt to sound a tonal response in a dozen others along the hall, like a cello vibrating to just one thumbed bass string. Not that the half dozen hungry members of the Lady's dancing chorus, as Cherry and May had discovered the first night, appeared to regard this side-line earning as anything to be embarrassed about afterward. The dogs across town in the Mexican settlement barked all night, too. Some night sounds were to be taken for granted.

Cherry said as much to May and added, "But somehow, the dogs don't bother me as much as — this other."

"The dogs are *supposed* to be bitches," said May. "Also the open air purifies some of the howling, I think, before it gets to you."

"Last night," Cherry murmured, resuming her brushing, "the big one at the end,

Lenora, ostrich feathers and spangles, you know, well — her bed fell *in!*"

"No need to tell me, *chalita.*" May pulled the gingham above her bare knees and sat on the edge of Cherry's cot. She gave an anxious study to Cherry. The paleness was still there, the eyes were too large and dark in their shadows, the hair-brushing a nervous outlet. She said, "I think Lenora must have been entertaining a Mexican cavalry squad. Horses and all. But I was a busy woman myself."

Cherry stopped brushing and turned. "The piano player again?"

"Eddie wanted a change in keyboards."

"What accompanist doesn't?"

"He's just like all the others we've ever known. Except this time he cottoned to the ugly duckling instead of the beauty. I guess he thinks Deputy Gomez has staked his claim for you."

Cherry grimaced. "What did he do?"

"I'm surprised you didn't overhear. This was all through the locked door. His general idea, well soaked in tequila, was that weren't we *both* artists and didn't I want to hear him hum a new composition he'd just dreamed up for us."

"I'll complain to Maceto!" Cherry stormed. "You didn't open the door?"

May nodded. "Only when he threatened to kick it in. He was all hands. You know how Eddie's fingers look at the piano below the footlights, skeleton bones scratching on a salt lick? Well, I had the little steel blade in my hand, and I just put the long ladylike tip of it to Eddie's stomach. That stopped the hands. I worked the point right hard to where his shirt was open and gave it a twist. Eddie left in a hurry."

"Oh — May!" Cherry abruptly put her face down in her arms on the dressing table.

"Don't do that, Cherry!"

"This awful place!" Cherry moaned from her arms. "It's practically a —"

"I know. But we've a job to do. You've been great, you *are* great. It's going to be all right. Just a few more days, now. Money — it's everything, at the moment. We've got to stick till we get a week's pay. It's all for Rusty, remember."

"Yes. As soon as we have money . . . Oh, I pray he is all right!"

May wandered restlessly to the window and looked down upon the Laredo back alleys. "The faces at night, and the smells . . . What I wouldn't give for just one breath of a good, clean hunk of dried-out, open prairie. just a little while longer . . ."

Cherry wiped at her tears. "May, you're

the strong one. Sometimes I feel that I'm unraveling. It's not knowing about Rusty, if he made it to that El Bar place."

"You're just tired. Look how well you did at the stage station. Nobody would have guessed —"

"I hope not. But you can't tell about that awful Navarro. I wanted to kill him that night!"

May watched Cherry beginning to dress. "Oh, I saw someone just now," she said. "I went to the balcony and looked down, to see if I might signal Ponch to bring us some coffee."

Freezing with her dress half buttoned, Cherry exclaimed, "Not Navarro!"

"No. The man who had the fight with Navarro. Dewey Lane."

"Here? In the Lady?"

"He was talking to a man and having a drink. They didn't see me, and I couldn't catch Ponch's eye without showing myself."

"We've got to find him," Cherry said excitedly. "He may know something!"

"Cultivate him, you mean? What would he know?"

"It's just a chance. He was going to El Bar, remember. Somehow, I think he saw straight through me."

"How could he? He and Navarro and everyone, they were seeing into you, Cherry, all right, but just what they wanted to see." She came over and put her mouth to Cherry's ear. "We'll happen to brush into Mister Dewey Lane and just happen to ask him what's going on, if anything, up the Laredo Road. Has he looked over his new El Bar place, for instance?"

Navarro rode back from the Tembler headquarters and detoured on his route to Laredo Road to hit the valley of El Bar. He digested all that Jake Tembler wrathfully had to tell him, and kept coming back to the tough meat that he had to swallow. Some man unknown had been in the El Bar shack, backing up Dewey Lane. A man without a face but with a lot of Winchester aim. Tembler had ordered him to get Lane off the El Bar claim. Then Tembler had ridden for Laredo, with Navarro detouring for a look at the El Bar place.

"Scare him off, whip him off, throw him in your damned jail — anything!" Tembler had said at the last. "Sorro will be sending two hundred Mexican mustangs up in another week. I've got to get to town to arrange for that, got them sold to an Army buyer at a hundred dollars a head. That's a twenty-thousand-dollar deal and I don't want this Lane squattin' there looking at it. Get him out. I can do it with my own bunch, but I don't know what connections the bastard may have. I got you to do it for me. You understand? Meet you in town this afternoon."

Now, as Navarro angled for the El Bar adobe shack, he thought he could kill two and maybe three birds with one stone. Lane would do for somebody to palm off on Sorro as the pal who had helped Rusty Ferris to escape. That would get rid of Lane at El Bar, take care of Tembler, soothe Sorro's hunger to shoot someone to avenge the death of his son. Carefully Navarro approached the house, watching for a sign of life. He pulled his carbine and went ahead on foot.

After finding traces of recent occupancy inside the cabin, Navarro developed an idea. He dragged in brush, piled it in the big room, and pulled the furniture around it. When all the wooden pieces were stacked, he touched fire to the mass and fanned the flames. The brush crackled, smoke drifted to the open windows, and the flames grew. The door caught, then Tembler's hard-built new porch awning, and fire shot through the back roof.

When Navarro rode down the valley toward the Road, he looked back a time or two, seeing the drifting smoke marking the place in the still valley. It wouldn't settle the whole thing, Navarro glumly concluded. But he brightened a little at the thought that it would give Mr. Dewey Lane the general idea. When he found Lane, and got him in a cell, he would gave him some more ideas.

But one question gnawed on. Who had been with Lane inside the adobe when they had made fools out of Jake Tembler and Hanson?

11

Within the first few minutes after Ed Carlos had introduced himself to Dewey at the bar in the Laredo Lady, the two hit it off like old friends. Dewey felt instant liking for the grizzled editor who had known his father.

"Peyton Evans told me," Carlos explained. "I knew your pa a long time ago when we were apprentice printers in Fort Worth. Understand you're from way-to-hell-and-gone somewhere in the Panhandle. Trying to start the El Bar spread. Well, you're taking a lobo by the tail, son."

"Go ahead and call me a damned fool. But that valley bit me, Carlos. I can run two thousand head of cows on that grass, and the market's not going to stay down forever. All the trails I'd ever follow would torment me if I didn't give El Bar a fair stab. That's how it is."

"Sounds to me like somebody's been selling you on this."

Dewey could have told him that a young

man with fevered tongue and wrists lacerated by handcuffs had sold him, partially at least, though he did not know where his own convictions and Rusty's build-up about El Bar had begun to support one another.

He said, "I've looked other owner's cattle in the rump on trail drives long enough. The world begins to be awfully empty when a man has no branding iron of his own that says this is the place he belongs."

"They call it land fever," said Carlos. "It's what'll build Texas if anything ever does. There's a breed that has got to match themselves against raw Texas land and every obstacle Creation can think of. You belong to that breed."

"Whatever it is," Dewey said with a hard grin, "my address will be that adobe house up at El Bar." Then he briefly told Carlos his troubles with Navarro and Tembler.

Carlos lowered his voice. "There's the first assistant to your friend Navarro, at the end of the bar. Name's Gomez, deputy sheriff."

Dewey glimpsed the chunky Mexican-featured man draining a beer schooner. Carlos added, "See the fish-mouth man at the table in the far corner, drinking with the two cowhands? That's the high sheriff, Haze Trevino."

"I don't think much of his choice of deputies."

"Those are Tembler hands he's sharing the bottle with. They'd be your neighbors. The young one with the sideburns is called Bo Apache. Tembler's hired gun, a mean kid."

On the sidewalk, Dewey remarked, "I've got a message to leave at the stage station."

"Suppose we meet at the hardware store after a while," Carlos suggested. "Maybe I can help you get some credit from Peyton Evans."

After he left his message at the station, Dewey continued along the shady side of Hidalgo Street which had thinned out at this time of day while most of Laredo drowsed through the long siesta pause. In the sunny silence, the light clatter of hurrying footsteps behind him came to his ears. He heard his name called.

"Dewey! Dewey Lane — wait a minute!"

Turning, he saw Cherry and May Gibbons coming, both in bright Spanish skirts and blouses, and Cherry with a ridiculous little parasol shouldered at a perky angle.

"We thought it was you!" Cherry exclaimed, out of breath. "Who else in Laredo has the stride of a fast horse — I'd as soon chase down a chapparal bird! *Whew* — were you running from us . . . Dewey?"

"You're the main reason I came to town." He took off his hat. Here was his chance to stake out the evening. Only problem was how to swing it in the presence of the watchful younger sister.

"It's almost like a family reunion, isn't it?" Cherry twirled her parasol.

"Yes, alumni of the stage station. All we need is Rusty Ferris —"

He saw the parasol slip from Cherry's hands. Retrieving it, he heard May speak dryly to breach the awkward moment. "How is your El Bar Ranch, Mr. Lane?"

He had to tear his gaze off Cherry. His thoughts about her probably stood out like a printed handbill. He tried to include the younger girl in his attention, for politeness. This was worse. May had the uncanny mind-reading look he remembered. Her directness trained on him, an inner shrewdness about his intentions. Funny how she made him feel transparent, this freckled-faced girl of no more than nineteen. Sure as hell that aloof little head of May's was secretly laughing at his chances.

Cherry had a way of forcing his attention back to her. "How long will you be in town? Surely long enough to see our show!"

"I intend to be there tonight." Belatedly,

he answered May. "El Bar is in fine shape. The house seems to need a woman's touch, though."

Cherry eyed him with hard brightness. "And the poor fellow who escaped from the deputy — I suppose he never was seen again?"

"He's probably half across the Indian Territory by now. Fellow like that wouldn't hang around long."

"I suppose not. You saw no trace of him at all?"

"No trace."

May murmured, "If you'll excuse me, I have an errand in the store," and left them.

He decided to throw for his point now, the dice having been rattled long enough. "I was thinking that maybe after your performance tonight we could get together. Just the two of us."

A shadow clouded Cherry's eyes even though the stage smile remained. "Would you tell me all about your El Bar place? You've seen so sign around there of Rusty Ferris?"

"Why would you ask that?"

"Oh, just curious."

"Suppose we get together after your show? Where are you staying?"

"Upstairs at the Lady."

161

"I'm listening for an invitation."

"Well, yes — I suppose so. It isn't much of a room — but we three could talk and —"

"Three's a mob."

She hesitated. "Well, you come to the show. We'll see."

"*Hasta la noche.*"

He concluded that he had his foot in the door.

May came out of the shop two doors down and rejoined them. Cherry found her smile again. "So we will look for you in the audience tonight. We'll sing a song just for you."

"That will be a real treat," May said straight-faced.

"I liked your *mañana* song," he said politely.

"It's better with a piano," said Cherry.

"We have a wonderful accompanist," May added.

The last thing he saw was May's expression, the way her tongue made a small point inside her mouth corner. Had he seen laughter, or mockery, or anger? The damned little sister bothered him like stinging nettle. As he moved off, he wondered if she was going to botch up his chances tonight with Cherry.

He angled across Hidalgo Street and a man came to his notice on the sidewalk, watching him. The man turned and padded between the swinging doors of the Star Saloon. Then Dewey remembered him, the deputy sheriff, Gomez, who had been pointed out by Carlos. Half-turning for a backward look, he saw Gomez emerge again, sided by a young man with long sideburns and wearing range garb. He recognized him as the Tembler hired gun, Bo Apache, who had been at the Lady with the sheriff. In the same moment, Dewey noticed the T brand on the horses at the tie rail. The same branch as he had seen on Tembler's and Hanson's horses.

He located Doc Orr's office and found the doctor just rousing from his siesta. His story there was that a transient rider had caught the accidental discharge of his own gun and badly needed medical attention. The doctor complained of the long miles to the stage station and then added that he would go as soon as he got his buggy hitched. Dewey handed him ten dollars.

When he returned to the hardware store, Peyton Evans invited him to the back office. Once more Dewey made his bid for credit for El Bar supplies. While Evans listened, he named what he needed — windmill parts. building materials for house repairs, wire for the corral poles, sundry equipment for the house, dynamite for building a creek dam. "I've got three hundred dollars cash — a little less by the time I leave town tomorrow. I'd like to hold on to some of it for hiring riders."

"You starting El Bar with just that?"

"That's right. But I can give a mortgage on maybe five hundred head of cattle with the El Bar brand. I don't know the exact tally yet. Then I'll be branding mavericks and adding them to the herd, fast as I can round them up."

Evans asked pointedly, "You think I could collect those El Bar cattle if I had to fore-close a mortgage?"

"I'd feel honor-bound to deliver them."

"How? Drive them right up Laredo, Road, with the Tembler crowd tipping their hats? They won't let you do it, Lane. Jake Tembler wants nobody on that land, and you and three hundred dollars are just no match for Jake's outfit." He aided gruffly, "Don't cross Navarro. Get rid of the idea and settle somewhere else. You wouldn't last a week at El Bar."

Dewey nailed him with a hard stare. More curtly than he intended he said "Am I keeping you from your siesta, Mr. Evans? I understand this is a population that likes to sleep."

Evans reddened. Nervously, he lighted a cigar. In a moment his mouth corner made a crooked smile. "You wouldn't be saying that I'm afraid to wake up, would you?"

Dewey stood. "You people down here ever hear of the Battle of San Jacinto? The rest of Texas won its independence then, and that was some years back. News must travel slow."

Evans growled, "Sit down!" He stretched his long legs far out. "Yes, the word has traveled slow. But I can tell you this, not everybody in Laredo is taking a siesta. Some of us are waking up."

Before Dewey could answer, the door opened, and Editor Carlos entered with no apology for the intrusion. "There's one of them, now," Evans grumbled.

Dewey told him, "Small world. Mr. Carlos knew my father. They learned the printing trade together."

"Well, Evans, you going to stake this fellow to what he needs for putting that ranch in shape, or has all your gambling blood turned to cider?"

"By God, I'm going to stake him," Evans snorted. "Send your wagon for what you need, Lane."

Dewey grinned. "Got no wagon, either."

"All right, I'll have to wagon it out there

for you. You tally your brand and we'll fix up a mortgage."

"You're smart, Peyton," Carios said.

"I'm a damn fool, you mean. Jake Tembler won't like me, but that's no love lost."

Dewey walked to the office door. "Thank you again, Evans. I'll bring in my supply list and cattle count in a few days."

"Oh, by the way," Evans said, stopping him with a frown. "What about grub, other stuff — I don't sell that. I'll tell you," he added, before Dewey could speak, "I'll arrange for that with Joe Crowder at the City Mercantile. It can all go into the same mortgage, and Joe and me'll agree on the details."

Dewey nodded, trying to hide his elation. Things were falling good, and damned fast, he thought, as he threaded his way out of the store's great jumble of merchandise. It was a start. All a man had a right to ask was a leg-up when he needed it, and then it was up to him to ride the bronc. Then he thought of Navarro, of Tembler, and his elation was gone.

In the store office, Carlos leaned back in a chair and blew cigar smoke to the ceiling.

"So he's going to tie into the Temblers and Navarro and everybody else, I reckon, with just guts and three hundred dollars. What'd you make of that?"

"I dunno. But he looks like he just might be the guy that could do it."

"Hadn't we might as well take him into our committee? Let him know what we're trying to do?"

Evans suggested, "Let's wait a little longer. Let's see how he makes out the first time he has a run-in with our fine Laredo law."

12

Dewey sighted the Barton camp in the grove at the wagon yard. He found Mrs. Barton seated in the shade of the wagon. She showed surprise, then pleasure, when she recognized him and urged him to sit and talk with her. "That's the worst of this place, I think," she said good-naturedly. "Not having anyone to talk with." She glanced at the slanting sun. "Joe will be back after a while. He's been off looking for work. "

"You people should be on cattle land somewhere," Dewey remarked to make conversation. "You don't seem to belong in a place like this."

"We've had our try. Several of them." Mrs. Barton looked at the surrounding squalor of nester camps. Quietly, and with no bitterness that he could detect, she said, "We've had to give up one claim after another. You have to understand how it was, Dewey. Joe was a city-bred man, and I was a school teacher, and here we've been all these years trying to pit ourselves against the mesquites and desert and longhorn cattle and Indian raids —" She sighed. "Then there came another problem. . . ."

As gently as he could, he said, "Such as a problem son, Mrs. Barton?"

Without meeting his eye, she asked, "Why would you suggest that?"

"No particular reason," he said carelessly. "I was one, myself. A son can be a problem."

"A son can be a source of pride and love," she corrected. "It doesn't matter what he does — at least not to his mother."

He looked down, turning his hat brim. "I reckon if I'd been in trouble, and if I was somewhere up the country here, knowing she would be anxious about me, I would try to send her word that I was all right. I think I would use a messenger I could trust, even if the messenger didn't quite understand what word I was sending to her. By the way, Mrs. Barton — the fellow who escaped, Rusty Ferris — I heard up the country that he might be hiding out around my place, somewhere on El Bar."

The dark-skinned woman brushed back her neat hair strands with a worn hand. "It's good," she said, "that he got away, and that a friend has helped him."

He matched her own restrained tone.

"And how would you know that, ma'am?"

She faced him unblinking. "One would assume that he had been given help."

"Assumed? Pardon me, but you spoke as if you knew."

"A woman develops intuition, I suppose, for things like that."

"A man my age develops intuition about caution." Dewey watched her narrowly. "The friend who helped Rusty Ferris risks going right along with him to a drumhead court in Coahuila."

For a time she did not speak, and then she searched over the whole frame of the big waiting man seated across from her. "The trouble here," she said uncertainly, "is how much to say, whom to trust. I don't really know you. It is too bad that God did not make our minds the organs that spoke to one another instead of our mouths."

"The Indians call it talking with two tongues."

"Yes. And how can one tell, do you suppose, which is talking?"

"I would say it called for mutual trust. Suppose two people had information they would like to trade, dropping all pretense. Each might be afraid. They would be risking their own skins and each knew that deception and treachery have a way of disguising themselves with forked-tongue words."

After a silence, a tired smile came to her sun-darkened face. "Dewey, you saw the horse hidden in the willows. Joe told me."

"Yes."

She reached across and touched his arm softly. "Will you wait until Joe comes? I would want my husband to talk with you now. This — you will understand that this is a responsibility I would not want to take alone."

"I'll be back."

There was one more concern behind her troubled eyes. "In this strange town, there is no law to turn to. We must be very careful."

As he approached the gate, he again saw the deputy, Gomez, near the corner of the yard office. This was no good, he thought. Gomez had seen him with the Gibbons girls, and with Mrs. Barton. Too much Gomez around for it to be accidental. A matter of time until his movements were reported to Navarro.

Gomez had hurried a block away, headed toward the jail, when Dewey came out of the grove. He tried to dismiss Deputy Gomez's sleuthing from mind. If Gomez had gone to relate his movements to Navarro, what could that self-admired tin star make out of it? Navarro might be mad the rest of his life about the fight at the stage station. But no trumped-up charge that Dewey had engineered Rusty's break would stand up two minutes in any court.

And if he got confirmation from Austin that Navarro had, as Rusty claimed, faked the extradition order, Dewey thought grimly that he would have ammunition enough to blow Navarro a mile high. Especially if he could ever find a Ranger or a U.S. Marshal, this far off the beaten track, to hand the information over to.

As he walked along, toward the City Mercantile, he had the feeling that Laredo was a freak animal, a captive town in the hands of the kingpins of two countries. A bastard settlement, in a way, sired by a sandy river and orphaned by the long desert distance to political-windy Austin. Sorro, the notorious czar of Coahuila, ruling a hundred miles of mountains on one side of the river, Jake Tembler in cahoots with him and the town law on the other side. This drowsy population of easily bought Mexicans and intimidated Anglos in between.

Dewey entered the City Mercantile, found Crowder, the owner, and learned that Evans had already arranged for credit. Crowder showed sober interest in Dewey's plans. "It's what we've been needing out at El

Bar," he commented.

It was arranged that Dewey's order would be filled when he returned to Laredo in a few days with his list of supplies needed from Evans's hardware store. For immediate grubstake, he left an order that could be packed north by horseback, which he would pick up in the morning.

On the street again, he let himself savor the satisfied feeling that he had achieved his first solid foothold for settling on El Bar. Evans and Crowder, and Carlos, too, had shown peculiar interest in his plans. For a stranger, up against the Tembler outfit, he was getting quite a parcel of store credit.

He headed for the hotel. He had been five hundred miles on a womanless trail. The Laredo Lady had whisky and he had money to buy it, and it had Cherry Gibbons, too. He was long overdue for a desert voyager's right to a mild drunk and the brush of calico. She had been the one to first flourish the deck. A healthy man would be a damn fool if he didn't offer to buy a stake of chips to see what cards she would deal.

Just before he reached the low walk in front of the Star Saloon he noticed the horses tied at the rail. Again he spotted the T brand.

He neared the center of the walk, opposite

the batwing panels of the small saloon. The doors suddenly swung outward. Two men emerged directly in his path. They made a show of stopping there, as if undecided.

Here was that chunky deputy, Gomez, again. And with him, Dewey recognized the Tembler rider with the long sideburns, drooping shoulders and tied-down gun holster.

He would have to walk into them, or wide around, the way they took up the center of the walk. He angled to pass near the saloon's batwings, feeling his neck burn and his armpits moisten. This had all the signs of a waylay and he was already in it.

"Ain't got one, Bo, but maybe this feller has."

"I'll just ask him, Gomez. . . . Friend, you got a match on you?"

Bo Apache slithered about in a weasel twist of movement, catching Dewey no more than a short stride from his slack-mouthed face with its little popped eyes.

Dewey felt his back brush the saloon's doors, his own quickening blood throb in his ears. He was braced by the pair in such a way that he could not back up unless he shouldered into the saloon. He took in Bo's dead, moist-mouthed face, Gomez's law badge, the street movement beyond the shaded walk. In the few seconds when he fumbled with his left hand in his pants pocket, he tried to figure the bracing in a bracket that fit, and could not light on any sane reason for Gomez springing it this way. Navarro's instructions?

He pulled out a match. "You got something to light with it?"

"Why?"

"You seemed to have forgot to roll your cigarette."

The youth took the match with dirty-clawed fingers. "I asked him politely, Gomez. Now he's tryin' to start trouble."

"No call for you to insult Bo," Gomez said. "He asked you for a match, civil."

"He's bigger'n me," Bo mumbled. His eye dots contracted to black pinpoints. "He's so big he even figures to take on the two singin' gals at once."

Now they would make their play. Dewey thought morosely. Here was Jake Tembler's own little killer. Here it had to come, whatever it was, and the prod was put together with such crudeness that the strings for it must have their pulling hands somewhere in the saloon behind him. Who was back there? Tembler? Hanson? He felt no surprise when the kid glanced past his shoulder, raised his woeful voice, and called,

"Hey, Hanson — Frank Hanson! There's a feller out here tryin' to start trouble with your best Tembler hand!"

He heard the heavy footsteps beyond the doors behind him. Dewey twisted. Frank Hanson loomed from the shadows inside. "Well, arrest him, Gomez. Do your duty. We'll talk it over with the gent down at the jail."

More than the threat of Hanson behind him turned Dewey cold in his veins, made each face, movement, and necessity stand sheathed in glistening clarity. Strangely what hurt was the insulting, degrading lack of subtlety. They were assured. They hadn't even bothered to dress up the trap.

Bo Apache prodded, "You think maybe you go so big with the singin' gals you own the sidewalk, eh? Like the big sister's bed upstairs . . ."

Dewey's back was half turned to Bo, who crowded behind him. It gave him extra momentum for his fast swinging turn. Hanson barked a warning too late. Dewey struck, triggering his leg muscles, his shoulder, his engulfing anger, everything blasting his stiff-armed fist solidly into Bo Apache's slack jaw. The knuckle bones of his fist smashed so hard that Bo's head snapped far back, his hat shooting high. Bo careened across the walk, past Gomez, glanced off an awning post, still staggering backward. He fell heavily where the hoofs of the tethered horses tangoed in anxiety.

Dewey slid against the wall to watch Gomez and to get his back removed from Hanson.

The nearer pedestrians halted, hypnotized by the twitching body of Bo Apache. Hanson stared from the batwings. Gomez had frozen into a knot.

In that fraction of time, Dewey bleakly watched the snakelike twist Bo Apache made in the dirt. The bloody mouth dropped full open. Bo worked his hand. Bo's gun cleared its holster almost before Dewey knew what was happening.

Bo half-raised on his left arm, his right hand leveled. The black snout of his revolver kicked. Dewey slid inches against the wall in a boxer's instinctive twist. The roar, the bullet splash, wood splinters, all came at one time. His mind worked at a crawl, it seemed to him, but warned that he was going to be killed, here and now, on a Laredo sidewalk. It said that Bo was the kind you couldn't merely hurt, you had to kill this kind or it killed you and there was nothing in between.

He barely knew how his own sixgun came

up flaming in his hand. It was out of his holster when Bo's shot splintered the wall beside him, and it flamed at its muzzle in a powerful kick of disgorging its load. This blasting roar in his hand, the sour smoke in his nostrils, became a part of the first shot from the street, one prolonged meeting of two compulsions to kill.

He saw the pulpy red socket spring up between Bo Apache's eyes, and he saw Bo lie down with the bullet hole pressed into the white dust. He had no more time than the split instant of seeing how a .44 slug hole looked in Bo's forehead. Then the Colt in his sweaty grip shifted its promise upon Gomez.

13

Gomez looked hopefully toward the jail, back again. He bleated, "Hanson, get your gun on him!"

Dewey whipped his .44 around. "Don't risk it, Hanson." People stared from little knots on the walk. Gomez flung a stuttered appeal to them.

"Why bother?" drawled Hanson. "We've got company — and the right kind."

Dewey whirled to see the two riders coming in a dusty gallop. Navarro and Tembler swung off their horses together, never turning their backs, their hand guns constant on the lone man backed to the wall, and he knew they had been somewhere near to witness this. They wanted one move, something to shoot him for, and Dewey read the purpose in their straining face muscles. He lowered his Colt.

"Drop it," Navarro said.

He let his gun thud to the walk.

Navarro stepped to the porch. Hanson

emerged now with his gun fisted.

Navarro looked both ways to see who made up the clusters of sidewalk witnesses. Tembler rolled over the body of Bo Apache. Navarro called, "Is Bo dead?"

"Right between the eyes."

Navarro smiled. "Now ain't you played hell, Lane?"

"Just ask these people, Navarro."

Hanson said, "It was cold-blooded murder."

"Cold-blooded as they come. I wish you had tried to run, Lane."

Dewey sought to find a face anywhere that would meet his eye and found none. "Didn't some of you people see him draw first, fire the first shot?"

Mexican faces stayed impassive. The Anglos shuffled their feet.

A portly man pushed through. "What's the trouble here, Navarro?"

"What'd you think, Sheriff?"

Sheriff Trevino worked his bloodshot stare over the scene. "This here's bad. How did it start?"

Navarro said, "We got it all in hand now, Haze. This one murdered the one down there."

"All Bo did," said Gomez, "was ask him for a match."

Dewey looked from Navarro to Tembler. "Which one of you planted it?"

Tembler said, "It's not going to make a damn bit of difference to you."

"It might to you when I get clear of this."

"What makes you think you will?"

"Because there's a bullet hole in the wall here. Your boy didn't make it after he was dead."

"Get him on to the jail," the sheriff told Navarro. "Some of you people pick up that dead man and carry him to the under-taker's. Bad sight, there in the dirt."

Navarro motioned with his gun. Dewey stepped off the walk. The long march across the weedy lots set up foot-plod drumbeats in his ears, measuring out his failures, and his error in thinking Navarro had no way to make trouble for him in Laredo.

Behind him, Navarro and Tembler walked abreast leading their horses, with Trevino a distance back. Navarro called, "How'd you like to make a little visit to Mexico, Lane?"

"Another extradition?"

Navarro started to answer, and Tembler said, "Shut up."

Dewey caught sight of Editor Carlos near the jail entrance. When the group came up Carlos said, "Trevino, I was standing in front of my office with a clear view of what happened. Under any damn law in Texas it was self-defense by Lane."

"Well, we're not having the damned trial here in the door!" Navarro gritted. "Get out of the way, Carlos."

Trevino cajoled, "Now, Carlos, no cause for you to give me so much trouble."

"I'm going to say in the paper that Dewey Lane was in good health when Navarro locked him up. He'd better come up for trial the same way."

"He'll get a fair trial," Trevino said.

"Did that man Davis get a fair trial?"

"He tried to escape —"

"He died from a pistol-whipping!" Carlos retorted. He looked hard at Navarro.

The deputy muttered, "Just keep messin' around, Carlos. . . . Get on inside there, Lane."

Carlos gave way. Dewey started inside. "Thanks, Carlos. I don't know any lawyer — could you —?"

Tembler said, "There ain't a lawyer in three hundred miles that'd want your case."

They took him along the corridor to a cell at the end. He heard Navarro's quick intake of breath and tried to dodge. Navarro's revolver barrel caught him a slashing blow at the base of his skull. The shock of pain staggered him. He felt his legs give, and lay conscious but unable to move. His brain tried to sift the meaning in talk drifting from the corridor.

Tembler was saying, "Can you get him across the river?"

Navarro cursed. "I'd as soon stomp the guts out of him."

"Well, you're the one Sorro looks to," Tembler said. "You'd better take him somebody to substitute for Rusty Ferris and try to square yourself."

The building became quiet. After a time Dewey raised his head to see the rotund shape of a slow-moving jailer pad past in the corridor, his string of keys clinking in his hand. The fat man rattled the door as he passed, testing the lock.

Dewey pulled himself up to the iron bunk. Sleep was the only escape from the pain.

The small high window was bright with another day's sun when he awoke. The back of his head throbbed wickedly. He recalled Navarro's words: "How'd you like to make a little visit to Mexico. . . ?"

The day wore on and nobody came. He was given one meal, sometime in the afternoon. The jailer slid a plate under the door containing frijoles, beef and bread. Dewey asked, "Where's Navarro?"

The big man shook his swarthy head. "No speek Englees. "

So Dewey asked it in Spanish. The jailer shrugged and replied in Spanish, "He had to go across the river today."

"Nobody came to see me?"

"You are not allowed to have visitors. Orders of Navarro."

Light dimmed in the window and dusk came quickly inside his cell. He wondered how Rusty had fared yesterday with Doc Orr. He remembered that Hagerman was to return Rusty to El Bar in a wagon. They would wonder why he had not shown up. The Gibbons girls probably would have heard by now that he was in jail. Hell of a date he'd kept with Cherry last night.

It was midnight in the Laredo Lady. The oil smoke of the footlights spiraled along the apron of the small stage.

Maceto, the proprietor, signaled to the round-shouldered man with the tieless stiff collar and black arm bands. "Hit it up, Professor." Eddie's long meatless fingers crouched over the keys.

"All right, ladies!" Eddie hissed. "Get your butts lined up and start kickin'!" He struck the keys. A drunk yelled, "Hoist the curtain!" A gaunt, underfed slat of a man in homesteader's patched denim eased out the front door. The man was gone like a shadow cast adrift from the lights and the music. The thin drift of him dissolved down an alley toward the wagon yard.

The drunk whooped again in the audience. The curtain went up. The bespangled chorus kicked red-gartered legs and broke into a raucous welcome song.

Navarro brushed through the swinging doors. He searched the crowd for a moment, then shouldered his way to stand beside Sheriff Trevino and Gomez at the bar. He downed two quick shots of whisky. Trevino inquired, "You been with Big Mex all day?"

Navarro nodded. "It's mean on the other side."

"How mean?"

"He counted on getting Ferris."

"But he'll take what'shisname?"

"Sí. He wants revenge. We're deliverin' Lane to him as the man that helped Ferris get away. It'll soothe Sorro's temper a little."

"When?"

Navarro braced himself for a third shot. "Tomorrow night. You seen Jake Tembler? Big Mex wants to set the time for that horse herd drive. It's ready to be crossed over."

Gomez said, "Tembler's in town."

Navarro turned his attention to the stage. "The sister's been on yet?"

"Ain't time."

Navarro muttered, "I think this ought to be my night with Cherry Gibbons. Tomorrow night we're deliverin' Dewey Lane across the border."

Trevino made a weak protest. "Don't you strongarm that girl. We got troubles enough."

He recoiled before Navarro's swift anger. The deputy gritted, "I get it any damn way I want it. Now shut your mouthin' and give me time to feel my whisky."

Gomez asked, "What'll Sorro do with him, Blackie? With this Lane guy?"

Navarro moodily watched the stage. "Firing squad," he muttered. He felt it coming on, that he was going to give Lane a good stomping before he tied him on a horse and delivered him to Sorro's bunch.

In the wings Cherry turned from a peephole and whispered to May, "Joe Barton has gone, and Navarro has come in. They're out there, all three. Joe will be making his try before long."

"Then it's up to us to delay the law here after the show."

"If it fails, May, we're in for some bad

trouble with Navarro."

"Don't worry, now. We've got to entertain those deputies long enough to slug them."

"Ponch will help. He promised me. May, you be careful. You be real careful when I'm gone. And when you collect our pay, you get out of here fast. Don't *ever* let Navarro or Gomez get you alone and don't —"

"I'll bring our money," said May. She bit her lip. "Cherry, I know you had to act — but why did you *never* give Dewey Lane a chance to look at me . . . just once!"

"You poor darling," Cherry whispered. "I didn't know —"

"Our cue!" May said. "Sing right straight to the Larado law, now!"

The voice in the night called softly, "That you, Lane?" Dewey could see nothing at the barred window. "Who's down there?"

"Is that Lane?"

"Yes."

A grating sound came through the bars. "You got it?"

Something hard touched his fingers. He clasped the stock of a small revolver. "Who are you?"

The voice came back impatiently. "Joe Barton. Listen now — set up a commotion and get the jailer down here, soon as I leave.

How you'll do it is up to you. Then hit for the wagon yard."

Barton was gone. Dewey fingered the little gun, small enough to have slipped between the bars. You're an old hand at this, Barton, he thought. Now he knew how Rusty must have felt.

He rattled the barred door and yelled, "Jailer! Jailer!" A lamp gave light somewhere. The fat man lumbered in sight, wearing only his union suit, and growled in Spanish, "What do you want?"

He put down the jailer's caution by turning his back. "Look at that bad gash in my head," he said pleadingly. "Got to have a doctor. Got to have it sewed up." The Jailer came close to the bars. Dewey grabbed him, his hand twisting into the fabric, and the gun snout poked deep into the soft stomach fat. "Unlock it."

In the corridor he shifted the gun to the jailer's back, pushing him ahead, worked a key to the lock in the center door, and then they were at the front. He changed the gun to his left hand. "Turn around!" He hit the jailer's limp jaw with a smashing uppercut. The heavy one sagged down. Dewey saw his .44 Colt on a table in the corner and grabbed it. Then he jogged into the night.

He trotted along an alley and went Indian-quiet to the wagon-yard gate. A shadow detached itself from a tree and whispered, "This way." They walked noiselessly through the silent grove, and Barton's wagon loomed in his face. Mrs. Barton said, "The place is fixed for him."

"Crawl under that stuff in the back," Barton directed. "Don't show your head and don't make any noise. We'll finish packing in the morning and pull out after daylight, so it'll look natural."

He lay in a black hole beneath a heap of the Bartons' possessions, nesting like a badger in a burrow. He heard no more sounds outside the wagon until daylight showed faintly through the cracks in his covering. After a time, he caught the sounds of the team being hitched, and of more gear being stowed in the wagon. Finally, he felt the jolt and sway of the wagonbed beneath him, the wheels rolling.

Hours later, Dewey blinked at the small shaft of sunlight showing at the end of his burrow. Someone had crawled back through the crowded cargo. Hands pushed aside the roof of his cover and a voice asked, "Are you all right, Dewey?"

He tried to struggle up, but his small cave was too cramped. "Who is it?" he demanded, knowing but disbelieving.

She said quickly, "It's *me*, Cherry. Are you all right?"

"What are you doing here?"

"We're taking you to El Bar."

"Lift some of this off me so I can get out."

"Not yet! Joe says just stay put in case we run into somebody searching for you."

14

After a long time the wagon began bumping over a rougher terrain, so he knew that they had turned off the Road. Unable to longer endure the cramped position, he pushed clear and surfaced above the tangle of household goods. The three in the wagon seat turned to look.

"Where are we?"

"El Bar land, now," Barton chuckled. "Your house is down here about three miles."

"How would you know where the house was located, Barton?"

"I was out here before. Found it in pitch dark once. Sighting you here scared me off."

"You needed a place for a rendezvous after Rusty got away. So it was the old El Bar house. That's where you intended to find Rusty, wasn't it?"

"You had us up in the air," admitted Barton. "I spied on the place but I was afraid to come too close."

Dewey asked sharply, "Why did you come, Cherry?"

Mrs. Barton spoke. "Cherry was trying to get information from you. We all were. You will understand that we were very worried and felt we had to be very careful in Laredo. You must realize how we have all worked at this every way that we could. Cherry and May in their way, Joe and I in ours. A life was at stake. No friend to turn to. What was done, we had to do ourselves. Over miles of strange country, with no money. I want to say — Cherry is not the kind of girl you think she is."

Barton, speaking no longer like a whipped nester, put in, "We're everlastingly indebted to you, Lane, for whatever you've done to keep Rusty out of Navarro's hands. Was he wounded?"

"Not bad," said Dewey, to minimize it. "I sent a doctor out."

Mrs. Barton said again, "I know you will understand — about Cherry."

"There's been a lot of acting going on. Nesters and show girls who just happppened to show up at the stage station." He was beginning to feel uncomfortable, thinking of the intentions he had exposed to Cherry.

Barton pulled up the team. "Look at that!"

Dewey twisted forward to see between the shoulders of Barton and his wife. He struggled from under the wagon sheet, over the side, and stood in the grass to stare at the ruins.

His El Bar house, what was left of it, was harshly lighted by the high sun. He saw a blackened mud hulk, everything burnable burned, the front wall caved in upon itself, the roof gone, smell of smoke and old embers fouling the air. The corral fence was reduced to a circle of charred poles, the shed an ash heap.

The Bartons and Cherry came to stand near him. Barton muttered, "They burned you out."

Cherry said, "Look! I *see* him!"

Dewey heard a sound like a choked-back sob. Mrs. Barton whispered, *"Rusty!"*

Dewey, in the same instant, sighted the two men in the clearing, near a wagon. A tall, stooped man, a smaller one. Both started walking, the smaller man waving his hand.

Cherry ran forward, her figure boyishly shaped by denim jeans and flannel shirt. Rusty detached himself from Hagerman's shadow and started jogging ahead in awkward motion, with one arm in a sling.

Dewey felt uncomfortably hot around his

neck and ears. *All I was trying to do,* he thought bleakly, *was to go to bed with her.*

Rusty stopped and opened his good arm for her, and Cherry melted into him, careful of his arm sling. Dewey swallowed the alkali in his throat. *Mañana comes soon, my Chula Chalita. . . .*

No wonder she and May had sung it to Rusty. Their message had been in the words, and right before Navarro's whisky-stoked eyeballs. *Mañana, they had warbled.* Cherry's love and a gun for Rusty in the night. He had paraded his intentions before both girls in Laredo like waving a banner, even mentioned his idea to Rusty, if he recalled right. Rusty had squirmed in the darkness, and no wonder.

Mrs. Barton touched his arm. He looked down into an expression of understanding. She nodded to the question he had not asked.

"You were right, Dewey. Rusty is our son."

"And Cherry —"

"Cherry is his wife. They had just married when Rusty took the job with the herd drive. He knew it was a Sorro herd, and that's why he changed his name to Ferris — for our sake, I guess. And money was *so* scarce."

"I know."

"That was the drive that ended in Mexico and got him in trouble."

Rusty called, "Come on down here!" Father and son hugged one another with no restraint, taking on like two drunks. Mrs. Barton followed more sedately, extending her arms, and Rusty twisted free and went toward her. She touched his cheek first, then kissed him. His good arm encircled her waist and held her tight.

Cherry said, "I couldn't stay away any longer, darling!"

The scene made Dewey feel an intruder, and he began to edge away, unnoticed until he stood near the unsmiling Hagerman.

"Howdy, Hagerman. I see you brought him back all right."

"Doc fixed him up. Wound was healin' better'n you thought. "

"He looks damned healthy."

"Been wonderin' what happened to you. We drove over last night. The boy was fit to be tied."

"I had a little trouble in town."

"You had some here, too." Hagerman frowned hard at the ruins.

"You bring my Winchester back?"

"In the wagon. Plenty of guns. Why?"

"This burning is meant as just a sample. I broke out of Navarro's jail."

195

"Stayin' here or leavin'?" Hagerman asked.

Dewey scanned the valley for sign, saw none, but wanted the carbine under his arm, anyhow. "Let's go down and see what's left to build back on."

Hagerman lumbered along, thought of something, and cast an owlish glance to Dewey as if bidding for approval. "Stage line's gone out of business, like I mentioned. They owed me back pay, so I helped myself to stuff in the station. Wagon's full of stuff." Carelessly, then, "Ain't got nowhere to go, nothin' to do with it. You need hands. Might could help a little."

And Dewey had his first ranch hand for El Bar. Barton caught up with them.

"Now as I see it," Barton said business-like, "yonder's all the building material we need for the time being, to get your house built back. Clay for adobe bricks. Need water, though. Means we'll have to get the windmill to working. Ought to be our first job. We can cut new poles for the horse pen after that. The women can live in our tent and attend to the camp chores till we get things fixed up —"

Dewey watched the eastern horizon. He detected a dark trace that was dust toward Tembler's. He repeated, "Did you say 'we'?"

"Sure." Barton's eyes twinkled when

Dewey turned to him. "Mama and Cherry are good at forming 'dobe brick. May, too, when she comes."

"May? She's coming here?"

"Soon as she can finish the week and collect their pay from Maceto. We needed every nickel we could get.

Benecke, that crippled stage driver, agreed to guide her out here. He'll bring your black horse."

Dewey turned his attention back to the dust smear. Riders out there, beyond the south Cibolo tree line. Barton went on, "We had to have an agreed place to get together, so 'way back there we set it for El Bar. Hope you can put up with us. We'll pull out soon as we can decide where to head and feel able to give Navarro the slip."

"I can put up with you." Dewey grinned. "Looks like I got an outfit and a family, all at one whack."

"Hey, Lane!" Rusty came trudging toward them, his arm about Cherry. "Did you get time to buy your fling in town? Hagerman, didn't we bring some whisky?"

"Didn't get the fling I expected, but I got enough," said Dewey shortly. Cherry was looking at him. He felt better when she laughed softly.

Dewey turned half of his attention to the

movement of riders toward the Tembler boundary. "I should have stayed in town and settled things with Navarro for keeps. Could be that's him yonder."

The dust of the riders had floated across the creek and stopped. He saw the far-off huddle, guessing they were pulled up for a caucus now. Plenty of time. Barton gazed across the valley and moved beside Rusty. "Son, did you ever see any prettier grass than that?" He said it admiringly, as if taking in the movements of a fine watch. "We could run two thousand head on that, if we had water for 'em." Not only was Barton not thinking of running; in his imagination he was off in the future, working a going cattle outfit with Dewey Lane. They needed May here, Dewey thought, to make it complete. He pushed the thought out, but it came back.

Hagerman came back with an armload of rifles and a whisky bottle. Dewey took his carbine and handed rifles to the others. They checked the loads. "Five riders in that bunch, I make it. What'd you think, Joe?"

"I count five. We could be lucky and they pack only sixguns, not expecting to run into a nest of rifles."

Dewey pulled the cork. "Let's hit this. then them."

"You first." Rusty winked. "It's your land. We're just trespassers." He kissed Cherry. "He's the torture merchant who dug the bullet out of me with a crowbar. Got the handcuffs off and sent Tembler and two of his men twelve mile home afoot. Most unpopular hombre on the border."

"I know." Cherry's gaze fixed Dewey with meaning. "I understand everything. Including lonely men, and long trails."

It was as if the past was now consigned to where it belonged. Dewey passed the whisky and levered his Winchester. "Ma and Cherry, get in the wagon and keep your heads down. The rest of us will spread out a bit and take cover before they ride in range. This is our land. I don't mean to give up what I've found today."

15

Frank Hanson spurred his horse ahead of his men and yanked his saddle rifle from its boot when Dewey stepped out. Hanson's purpose changed abruptly. His neck craned as he counted the muzzles of three other rifles trained on him from the trees. Dewey held his rifle half-raised and called, "That's far enough, Hanson. What's on your mind?"

What was on the foreman's mind, now showing, was that he was caught in a trap. Rifles he hadn't expected, and his men armed only with short-range hip guns.

He muttered, "Thought you was in jail."

So the Tembler headquarters had not received the news yet. Dewey said, "You left town too soon. I got acquitted."

Hanson called uneasily, "Who's that in them trees?"

"The El Bar outfit."

Hanson glanced back at his uneasy riders, around again at the rides showing. "You wasn't satisfied, Lane, when you had a whole skin. Jake and Navarro are goin' to be right interested in this." Hanson talked too much. In his bluster, he let his tongue run too loose. "If they wasn't across the border on business a few days, you'd be taken care of mighty damn permanent."

"Sorro crooked a finger and they went running? Is that it, Hanson?"

The foreman scowled. He showed a sudden itch to ride away, as did his companions. He flung a final threat. "You take some good advice, feller — drag out of here, fast, while you can."

"*Adiós,* Hanson. You earned your pay. You spoke your piece. Now head your boys for home ground and don't come back. Especially don't ride down this valley in the night."

Hanson gathered his reins. He took one final look around, muttered, "Let's go," and struck out at a lope on the back trail, his riders crowding him.

Rusty joined Dewey. "Only a matter of time now, I reckon."

"Nobody's obliged to stay for the trouble if you don't want to."

"Well, you're staying, aren't you?" demanded Rusty.

"It's my land."

Joe Barton put a hand on Dewey's shoulder. "You talk like a Barton feels.

When a man can't stand up for his own property in Texas, they can shovel the clods on me. My gun, though, will be red hot when they do it."

During the next two days, while Rusty stood lookout on the rise back of the windmill, Dewey, Barton and Hagerman worked cattle from dawn to sundown. They flushed wild longhorns out of the brush, attempting to get a tally. They worked with attention alert for sign of riders toward Tembler range or west toward Laredo Road.

Dewey told them it was like living on borrowed time. If he could only complete a tally of his brand, somehow get into town without trouble, get his load of supplies, hire two or three more riders. The daily labor afforded little time for talk. The Bartons, Dewey surmised, had managed to bring themselves to date on their various past experiences. But the gaps were not filled in for Hagerman and him until the second night.

They were reclining about the campfire, dead-tired all, when Dewey overheard Cherry mention May's name. Cherry said worriedly, "Tomorrow is payday at the Lady. I hope she can draw our money and leave without trouble. I'm so worried about her, alone in that place."

"May was never afraid of a thing in her life," replied Rusty.

"I know. All the time, while we were traveling south to try to keep up with you, she was the brave one. She was the one who insisted I act like a show girl around Navarro. And, Rusty, did you know she practically slugged Navarro and Lenman with whisky that night in the station?"

Dewey said, "I wondered about that. No wonder Navarro and Lenman were so shaky when Rusty walked out with that gun in his hand."

"It all helped," commented Rusty.

"Another thing," Dewey remembered, "Cherry bumped into Navarro when he headed for the door after Rusty. Made it look like an accident, but you slowed him up. I remember several things now. But you've never told me how it all started, how far back and where."

Barton said, "My wife and I were on the move to a graze out at Angelo when we got word from a friend that Rusty had been jailed there. Cherry and May were singing in Sonora. Sorta by mutual consent we all drifted to Angelo, soon as we could. I reckon you can understand, Lane, that we've been a close family, one to stick up for our own. But we never had any money. Cherry and May had tried for singing jobs while Rusty went off and changed his name and got on that cattle drive to Mexico. Everybody was doing the best he could to make a dollar. When we got the bad news, we just dropped what we were doing and collected as near Rusty as we could, trying to hit on some way to get him out of the trouble. I got just a minute, one night, to talk to him at the window of that Angelo jail. But no chance to do anything. They were railroadin' him to certain death. It was up to us to stop it."

"Navarro and Lenman were keeping a close watch," Rusty explained. "All we had time to agree on was that the folks would drift south, same direction as I was going. And try to spring me somehow."

"All we knew," Mrs. Barton added, "was that if they ever got our boy across the border we would never see him again."

Dewey asked Cherry, "Did you and May actually have an engagement at the Laredo Lady when you took the stage south?"

"No. We made that up, but we had no trouble getting booked when we applied there. The main thing, you see, was our need for money."

Money is the thing, all over Texas, Dewey

thought. So many in the same fix. Plenty of beef and land, but no dollars. So there was a family, the flat-broke parents and two girls, playing tag with the Laredo law and their captive, all moving bare-handed across the desert miles from Angelo, intent on somehow reclaiming their own before he vanished into the hills of Coahuila. He heard Hagerman mumble a question. "Which one smuggled him the sixshooter?"

"I did," Barton replied. "In the blackest part of the night, through that window. And a chisel, too. Longest five minutes in my life, going up there. The chisel was in case he ran on to anybody who would be willing to work it, in case I got delayed finding him at El Bar."

"The gun was in my valise," said Cherry. "When the rest of us went down to look at the crossing, May hid the gun in her dress and went to the wagon camp, so Joe had a gun to slip to Rusty."

"The longest five minutes," Mrs. Barton corrected, "was when I went up and let the stock out of the pen that night while Joe kept watch on the house."

Cherry had her own version. "Singing that song was my longest five minutes. Navarro's horrible stare on me."

Hagerman laughed hoarsely. "Bunch o' Indians couldn't of done it better. You want to know what I liked best, it was Lane here beatin' thunder out of Navarro. Till Navarro up with that bottle."

"You were to meet Rusty here, Joe?" Dewey asked. "At El Bar?"

"Yes. It was all the plan we had time to make. Rusty knew there was an abandoned shack here, mentioned it in Angelo. Meeting place for us if we needed one. We went on to Laredo to keep Navarro from getting suspicious. I looked for jobs days. One night I rode out here and saw your light in the house. Didn't know what to do except sweat it out and wait to see what you aimed to do with Rusty."

Cherry said, "May and I hoped to get you to talk, Dewey. Joe had a pretty good idea by then that you were not going to turn Rusty back to the law. We had plans for the other night, to draw you out. . . ." Dewey shifted uncomfortably, hoping that she was not going to say too much in front of the others. She went on casually. "Turned out you didn't keep the date for the very good reason that you were in jail. So we made our plans, and that night we entertained Navarro and Gomez while Joe did some gun smuggling again. May and I sat with Navarro and Gomez in the Lady after the show. Every time they started suggesting we go to our rooms, we signaled Ponch to bring some more whisky."

Thinking back, Dewey realized that there was a plain trail behind them for Navarro to see. "He knows I talked with you, and with Joe and Ma. He'll soon link all that up with my escape."

Rusty said harshly, "Our troubles all start back with Sorro — till I get that *bastardo* in my gun sight I'll never be able to sleep easy the rest of my life."

"Now, son," Barton cautioned, "there's such a thing as taking on something too big to handle."

They were all silent for a while. At last Dewey said, "When our trouble comes, it could be one of two ways. Sorro's outfit might try to deliver a herd straight across our land as the easiest way to get to Tembler's place. Or Navarro might bring in the Tembler bunch and hit us from the east. When May comes tomorrow, there'll be three women here and I don't like the idea of exposing them to what's likely to happen. Here's my idea. Hagerman, since the stage line is out of business, what about a move to the stage station for new headquarters? Soon as I can make the contact in town, I would like to see if I can take over the station layout which would be perfect for a new El

Bar home place. Maybe trade for the stretch of land, too, connecting up the valley here with the stage station property, making one big spread out of it. Have to be on credit, but the stage company probably has no more use for the property. That way —"

Barton chuckled. "Ambitious, for a broke man — but like you say, it would be a perfect ranch headquarters."

Hagerman nodded. "The company would sell it cheap and take a mortgage, likely."

Dewey rose and lifted his rifle. "My job now is getting into Laredo with our cattle count and trading for supplies. Also trying to deal for the stage station. If I can do that, and hire two or three more riders —"

"We would still have Sorro, Navarro and Tembler," Rusty cut in.

Dewey peered off into the night. "You took the words right out of my mouth," he murmured.

He walked away to begin the first night watch. Behind him, he heard Barton say, "Well, Hagerman, we better get some sleep. Tomorrow we got that cussed windmill to whip."

Mrs. Barton called, "Dewey — you be real careful out there."

"Sure will . . . Ma."

He took his stand in the brush on the rise

behind the burned house. In some way, as natural as the stars slipping out, he had acquired himself a family, ranch hands, friends, all in one strangely assorted group. Six, now instead of himself, alone, when Jake Tembler and Navarro made their move to dislodge the new owner of El Bar. Tomorrow, they had said, May was coming with Benecke as her escort to show her the way to El Bar.

The mocking, penetrating appraisal he had last seen in May's eyes came back to mind, causing him to shift uncomfortably. But he knew he was worried about May. She was alone in Laredo. Navarro might have linked him up to the Bartons and the Gibbons girls after his escape. Tomorrow he had to go into Laredo. He would move this outfit to the stage station, and go into town alone. Either he would meet May and Benecke on the way out, or find May in town. And he would try to make his deal for supplies and for buying the stage station property.

Could he do that and still dodge a meeting with Navarro?

As he speculated on this, his ears caught sound of an approaching horse. Coming from the west, from Laredo Road. He slipped down the incline, keeping to cover. The sounds came nearer, turned, and headed directly toward the camp. Dewey stepped from behind a cedar and leveled his rifle as the rider and a led horse took shape in the dark.

"Hold it!"

"That you, Lane?"

"Yes. Who are you?"

The figure separated from the saddle and advanced in a hobbling walk. "I'm Benecke."

"Where's May Gibbons?"

"Afraid I got bad news. Her sister here?"

"Damn it, Benecke, what's happened?"

Benecke let out a tired sigh. "Navarro got her. She's in jail. Or somewhere. Navarro figured out the Gibbons girls and the Bartons had something to do with your jail break. Cherry gone sudden from the Lady, Bartons gone sudden from the wagon camp. See? So he nabbed all that was left. May Gibbons. Something more that that, I found out. It'll turn your stomach."

"It's already turned. Go on."

"Ponch, the head barkeep at the Lady, is a friend of mine. Ponch hears and sees a lot. Some of Sorro's men saw the girls in their act at the Lady. Ponch heard 'em talkin' about how Sorro would like those two girls."

Benecke went silent. Dewey's mind fought against the thing that Benecke's words, and now his silence, suggested. "No!" he protested hoarsely. "Navarro wouldn't —"

"Navarro works for Sorro," said Benecke simply. "If he had need to put himself in good with the Mex bandit, there was his way."

"He had the need," Dewey said numbly. "He owed Sorro the return of Rusty Ferris."

"She might be in jail," muttered Benecke, "or she might be across in that Casino dive in Nuevo Laredo, where Sorro throws a fandango once in a while. I picked up your black and another horse today, ready to bring May out here, but she didn't show. That's when I scouted around a little. Ponch told me what I'm tellin' you. Navarro had caught her with her valise packed and took her down to his damned jail. I reckon he knew what he wanted to do with her."

Dewey felt sick. May Gibbons. The young one, the shrewd, sensitive, silently amused one, with her small-girl freckles and no fear of the world. But she would know fear now. Why had they left her to fall into such a trap? Bitterly, beneath his breath, he cursed himself, and all the rest, and then this died off. His mind settled steadily upon the things to be done.

Because Benecke had made the ride, had done his best, he said, "Thanks for coming, for bringing my horse. Tell it to them easy down here, will you? These are her folks. They're apt to do any crazy thing when they know."

"You goin' it lone-handed?"

"The only way. Indian-footed, no brass hand."

"What if she's been strong-armed across the river to entertain that bandit?"

"Then I cross the river."

"Want a suggestion for a place to start?"

"I'm willing to listen."

"Start at the weakest link and work from there."

"Which is — ?"

"Haze Trevino."

"The high sheriff?"

"He could be made to talk. If you was willin' to do a little knife work on him if he balked."

Dewey smiled crookedly, thinking that would be easy, easy and welcome and no pain to conscience, if they had harmed May. "*Bueno.* I start with Trevino. I've no better plan. All I want is to find her."

"The time Navarro stomped me in jail, just because I was drunk and sassed him, Trevino he got sick at his stomach. You get

Trevino where you can do a little Apache carving on his beauty, he'll turn wrong side out with talk."

"Does he live at the jail?"

"No, in a house not far from it. By hisself, except when he has a Mexican *puta* there."

"Thanks, Benecke. Now break it easy to the family here."

Benecke told it that May merely had failed to appear, and fumbled a little in the telling. Rusty, first, then Joe Barton, assaulted him with questions. Dewey intervened. "Take it easy, now. I'm riding in to find her. Probably nothing wrong — likely we'll be back by sundown tomorrow. You load these wagons and move back to the stage station. Better there than here, if Tembler and Navarro hit. Benecke, will you stay with them?"

"Got nothing better to do."

Rusty stooped to pick up a saddle. Dewey moved, pressuring down his booted foot on the seat. "What's the idea?"

"I'm riding to Laredo with you."

"Just me. Tell him, Joe, that he's in no shape for it."

"Dewey is right," Barton had to admit. "We could all go, but we would just attract attention, likely land in jail, or worse. Let him have his try, Rusty."

Rusty gritted his displeasure. "If you're not back with her by tomorrow afternoon —"

"Then we'll both go," Barton said.

While he was saddling his horse, Cherry came over and murmured, "Tell me the truth, Dewey. Has Navarro — ?"

"Benecke didn't say," he lied hastily. "Maybe it's nothing at all."

She murmured her disbelief. He left the group standing in a silent huddle and headed on a short cut for Laredo Road. He could make the ride before midnight, he reasoned, and do what he could by daylight. At that, he might be too late. Too late for what? He touched spurs to set the black flowing in a ground-covering gallop. Navarro had a mania to stomp or pistol-whip a male prisoner he happened to dislike. What did the crazy deputy do with a female prisoner?

The Road slid under him, the tracks wound southward, reaching always ahead into the hazy starlight and to his coldly decided purpose for the end of his ride. If Navarro had harmed May Gibbons, Navarro had to pay. The slow way. Then die.

16

The darkened town nested in the purple coil of the Rio Grande. He entered the outskirts, trying for silence on a sandy back street. He heard horses, two or more, coming behind him, but these sounds soon faded over on Hidalgo while he waited. He rode on to the west fringe of the business section. Dismounting, he proceeded afoot through a rutted alley, far enough to get a look at the main street. Southward, horses showed at the rails along saloon row and in front of the Laredo Lady. The upper end of the business street was deserted. Yet one crack of light escaped and this pulled his attention to the back office window of the hardware store.

His scrutiny was altered by a small shadow of movement beyond the store light. Someone appeared to move afoot, but not like a man walking upright. Whatever it was, the shadowy outline dissolved into nothing. He could not tell whether it had emerged from the back of the store, or had entered the rear door. The crack of light at the window was gone.

Dogs barked southward in the Mexican quarter. Three men came from a saloon a block away, untied horses at the rail, and were swallowed in the night toward the river. Dewey retraced his way out of the alley. He led his horse until he came to the trees near the wagon yard where the Bartons had camped. There he stopped again, tied the black, studied the dim shape of the distant jail building, remembering his dismal time inside its adobe wall.

Was she in there? The dark walls looked solid and impregnable. They looked what they were, the stout enclosure hiding a ruthless man's way of handling his enemies. Dewey worked his gun loose momentarily, half drawing it, then firmed it down again, sliding his holster to a hang he liked, and moved one numb leg after another in a slow walk. A dog trotted out of the weeds, growling.

Dewey walked on. At last he pressed his body hard against the jail's wall settling there to wait and listen. The dog stopped a distance out and sat on its haunches.

Two riders came, trotting their horses across the front of the lot. They dismounted and advanced to the doorway out of

Dewey's sight, talking carelessy.

"Gomez! Hey, Gomez! Open up!"

He heard the answering voice inside. "Who is it?"

"Hanson and Rollins. Open your damn door."

Gomez opened the door. Hanson said, "We just got in. The big deal all set?"

Gomez said, "Yeah, at the west crossing. They're all there but you, and you better get a move on."

"What time's the herd comin' over?"

"Sometime before daylight. Sorro's boys was holdin' the bunch on the south side around sundown. Two hundred mustangs ain't no picnic. Navarro and Tembler said get out there *pronto.*"

"Yeah. Well, I got plenty of news for them. Something's happened while they been down in Mexico. C'mon, Rollins, our work's cut out, movin' them horses."

"What kind of news?" Gomez wanted to know.

"The guy that broke jail. Lane."

"That so? Where'd he vamoose to?"

"He's holed up at El Bar. Him and at least three more and they ain't goin'to be as easy to move as Navarro might of thought. Plenty of rifles. Two wagons. I been waitin' for Jake and Navarro to get back from

Sorro's place to see how they want to take him."

Gomez whistled. "You better high-tail for the crossin' and tell Navarro. Wonder if the girl is with'em?"

"What girl?"

"Cherry Gibbons. She took out same time Lane made his break. Navarro nabbed the other one, the sister."

Hanson asked curiously, "What did he do with her? You got her inside?"

"Nope. Not now. But that's Navarro's business."

Hanson chuckled. "Some business. The high sheriff around?"

"Home drunk. Started gettin' a load on when he found out the delivery was set tonight. Haze is nervous as a mare, says the Citizens Committee is prime to start trouble. You know how Haze —"

Rollins grumbled, "Let's go, Frank."

"All right. Look at that damn dog, actin' like he's cornered a cougar. See what's around the corner, Rollins."

"Aw, hell, we better hit for the crossin', we ain't got all night."

Dewey drew his gun. The dog trotted a few steps after the departing pair, and, when they mounted, padded back to the corner. Hanson and Rollins rode out of hearing.

The dog growled, and Dewey realized the jail door had not yet been closed. He moved out from the wall, the dog backed off, barking. Gomez mumbled something. Dewey heard his movements as he came down the steps.

They met at the corner, two shadows a dark collision between the deputy's stomach and the muzzle of Dewey's raised Colt. The dog rushed this way and that, barking excitedly.

Dewey backed Gomez all the way to the door, into the corridor, and took the deputy's gun as the office-light reflection fell on his face. Gomez turned, showed recognition, and grunted sickly.

"Walk ahead of me. Keep reaching high."

All the cells were empty. *I'm too late,* Dewey thought.

"Where is she?"

"I swear to God. Lane, I don't know —"

"Does Trevino know?"

"He might."

Dewey muttered, "The weak link." Aloud, "We go now, Gomez. No sound, no sound at all."

Gomez moved carefully ahead of Dewey's gun and out the door. "What you doin' with me?"

"The high sheriff's house. You show me

the way. One little move, and you're done for."

Gomez mounted his horse and after Dewey found and remounted the black they rode a short distance, coming out in a scattering of houses west of the jail. Gomez mutely led him upon the dark porch of a frame structure. "What're you carryin' that coil of rope for?"

"Knock. Talk natural."

Gomez said over his shoulder, "Trevino's mighty nervous tonight, Lane — he's apt to do somethin' wild as not — I don't like —"

Dewey reached past him and knocked. After a long wait a light showed. "Who's out there?"

Dewey pressured the gun into Gomez. Gomez called his name. "Need to see you, Haze."

Trevino opened the door. He staggered back as Dewey pushed Gomez inside. Trevino had pulled on his pants and belted gun. One word gushed out of his mouth as his eyes protruded. *"Lane!"* In the same instant, Gomez yelled, "Look out!" and whirled. Trevino's whisky stupor exploded into panic. He fought out his gun, and Dewey saw that both of them had completely stampeded. He slapped hard at Gomez, who had missed his lunge at

Dewey's gun hand, and cuffed him sharply erect, powering Gomez back in front of him. The short pudgy body rocked as it took Trevino's wild shot.

Gomez slapped both hands to his chest, murmured, *"No, Haze . . ."* and began to sag. As he went down, Dewey smashed his Colt across Trevino's wrist, and the sheriff dropped his smoking gun, caught his dangling right hand, and went into high-pitched cursing.

"Turn Gomez over."

Trevino did so, one-handed. He cringed. "My God, I killed him!"

"You didn't kill much."

Dewey kicked the door closed. "If that shot brings anybody, you'll say that your gun just went off. Talk fast, now, Sheriff. Where is the girl?" He glanced at Gomez's body with distaste, felt nothing but distaste for the other one, the cowering, whisky-reeking man with the weak eyes who still clutched his broken wrist. A cold, detached disbelief seized him as he realized that he could go ahead and do what he had to do with Trevino. The lie, the evasion, began to show in Trevino's dull stare. The sheriff numbly shook his head, wet his lips.

"Where's the girl?"

"I dunno — what's the rope for?"

Dewey stepped past him. Trevino could not turn as quickly. Dewey flipped his Colt, changed his grip, and smashed the butt down upon Trevino's skull. He caught the man under the armpits and stretched him in a corner of the room and got to work with his rope coil, cutting it to shorter lengths. He brought water from the kitchen, after he had finished, and poured it on Trevino's face.

He watched impatiently until Trevino had finished his first flurry of desperate struggling.

"What've you done to me?" Trevino lay still, exhausted.

"You're spread-eagled, Haze. Spread-eagled and naked."

He watched, steeling himself against the ugliness of it while Trevino struggled again, and understood a little what the Apaches got out of it, how a man tied with his arms and legs spread-eagled and naked suffered the worst sense of helplessness, the most lonely feeling in the most tormenting fix a man could know. Dewey made his fingers open his long-bladed knife. He squatted beside the body that had spent itself, now wracked with hard breathing.

"Where's May Gibbons?"

Trevino locked his eyes to the knife. He

groaned, "Across the river."

"What place?"

"The Casino. In Nuevo Laredo . . . for God's sake, Lane . . ."

"Sorro's hangout?"

Trevino nodded vigorously.

"Did Navarro — did he bother her, before he took her over?"

"No. I swear he didn't. Sorro wanted her for a fandango." Trevino was covered with sweat drops. He tiredly flung his head from side to side, as if dying of a fever.

"What about the herd delivery? How many men? How will they do it?"

Trevino squirmed. Dewey ran the flat of the cold knife steel lightly up and down Trevino's flabby stomach.

The sheriff moaned. "Navarro and Tembler are takin' delivery. West crossing. Tembler's crew, about fifteen men. Sorro's bunch drive 'em to the river . . . Tembler's bunch brings 'em over. . . . Hold this side till tomorrow night, then drive to Tembler's place."

"Sorro's celebration, when does it start, how long does it go on?"

"After the delivery, goes for two or three days sometimes."

"You're an ugly bastard, Trevino, even with clothes on — but not as ugly as I've a mind to make you now with this blade. What if I gave you a chance? Put away my knife, let you dress — would you be thankful enough for keeping all your parts inside you to get me across the river, talk us into that Sorro fandango?"

Trevino groaned. "You'd get us shot over there."

"A bullet over there, or a knife here. Which?"

"I'll go. Lemme up."

The gamble was no good. Dewey stood and moved about and fought with his own indecision. The chances were too slim. *What could I do over there in the middle of Sorro's crowd?* He stared blankly at Gomez, dead and ugly on the carpet. *Why do I have to be the one to find May Gibbons?* Gomez's dead lips whispered back, *Because she's little more than a kid, she's freckled, she looked at you with that look you were too damned slow to understand.* He rubbed an unsteady hand across his eyes. *I have to do it.* She was over there, no more than three miles from where he stood with a dead man and a spread-eagled naked sheriff, and Navarro and Tembler and their men would not be gone forever with that Sorro herd. If it was going to be bad for her, where they had taken her, at least she might sometime know, and maybe it would be worth a little to her, at the last . . . that he had crossed the river. That she had not been alone. That he had tried. To Trevino he said, "My gun will be on you all the time. Botch me up with them over there and you get it first." He started slashing the ropes that stretched Trevino like a hide on a wall.

The sheriff had struggled to all-fours, and Dewey was kicking his clothes across to him, when the footsteps clattered across the porch. They came on loudly, and a fist banged against the door.

"Trevino! Hey, wake up in there, Sheriff! Open up!"

Dewey clapped a heavy palm over Trevino's mouth. He whispered, "Ask who it is!"

Trevino called weakly, "Who's out there?"

"Bill Elston and Figuero. You better move fast — there's trouble."

Dewey whispered, "Ask them what kind of trouble." The sheriff repeated his words.

"That citizen's bunch — they're on the move. Gomez has disappeared and your jail is wide open — come to the door, you damned drunk old —"

"Bust it in, Bill."

A heavy shoulder jolted the front door. "Hit it again. . . . Damn it, Trevino — we're tryin' to warn you. You got to get word to Jake."

Dewey did not wait for the next smash against the locked door. He ran at a crouch for the kitchen, and fought the stubborn fastening of the rear door. Trevino raised his voice at last in a high yell for help. Dewey heard the front door smash inward as he made it to the outside darkness.

A gun immediately blasted in the night. The slug smashed the doorway to his left, showering him with splinters. *Damn it, why would Trevino's friends surround the house?*

He dived to the side for a vault over a low porch railing. A confusion of voices and sounds came from behind in the house, as well as outside in the darkness, seemingly from everywhere. Then he was falling, out of balance, his foot tangled in a mass of clutching vines.

Fire and blackness rose up together to stagger him. Dazed but conscious of a gun roar, of a bursting flare of pain in his side, he lay sprawled, groping with his hand for his gun lost on the ground. He clawed at earth, weeds, gritting his teeth against the pain in his ribs. He suffered a nightmarish confusion of sensations — that he was shot, that the men were gunning him from inside the house but that the bullets were coming from the darkness of the yard.

He knew an engulfing tiredness and gave up feeling for his gun. He put his hand inside his jacket, where a ripped place felt soggy with blood. The lead slug nested shallow there, in his ribs, and he pressured it out, blinding himself with the pain of it and not caring that he had to give way to something like drugged sleep. . . .

The voice, after a dreamy eternity, floated from above him. "There's one down there in the weeds — watch him, now."

A match flared. Dewey closed his eyes against the glare.

"My God! It's Lane!"

"Who's he, Carlos?"

Dewey tried to fight off the hands that lifted him. "Hello, Mr. Carlos." That was all he could manage before lapsing into sleep again.

The morning sun poured through a window. One by one, the faces in a room etched into focus. Ed Carlos, Evans, other men he had never seen before. Doc Orr, standing at the window, smoking a cigar. The sunshine hit his eyes from the window's iron bars. *The jail!* He struggled up and stood beside his cot.

"Do that again," Doc Orr said, "and

you'll have to be sewed up all over."

Dewey sank back to the cot edge. "What happened?"

"You caught a ricochet bullet in your ribs, not deep but mean enough."

Editor Carlos said, "We've taken over the jail, got Trevino and two of his pals locked in his own cells. This time tomorrow we hope to have all the cells full and prisoners two deep on the floor."

Like the other men, Carlos looked very grim, with red, sleepless eyes, a whisker stubble, two sixguns weighting his cartridge belt. He came over and sat beside Dewey. "Just what the hell was it, Lane? Trevino naked, Gomez dead, Bill Elston and Figuero gunning after you, and you passed out in a jungle of honeysuckle vines?"

"Odd thing," Dewey murmured, "very odd thing." Then, "What the hell were you pulling off there, outside Trevino's house?"

"Last night we got my crowd together — these men, some others, the Citizens Committee that's fed up with the election frauds and the law's tie-in with Sorro. We met in Evans's store last night and decided to hit while Navarro and his main force were handling a horse-herd delivery from Sorro. We meant to take Trevino and Gomez, all the others we could round up in town, then lay for Navarro and Tembler, catch them red-handed. Somebody must have spotted us congregating last night. Bill Elston and Figuero beat us to Trevino's house, where we had intended to make a quiet nab, get him and Gomez locked up. All the others we could pounce on, before word leaked out to the men at the crossing. We surrounded the house and hit. Moved in on the damnedest sight imaginable in the sheriff's front room. Then some of our men at the back saw you taking a dive over the back porch and damned near picked you off with a rifle. We hauled in Trevino, and Elston, his brother-in-law, and Figuero, and Gomez, dead, and you bleeding white."

Dewey digested it, looking from one hard-drawn face to another. Carlos called off their names and their identities, winding up with, "And that's Lige Fitzpatrick over there, owns the Sonora stage line, except Lige has hit bad luck and gone out of business. There are about thirty others on our sicle."

Dewey stared at the small, sun-reddened man named Lige Fitzpatrick. He tried to remember something that was important. "The Sonora stage line — you closed it down, didn't you? Something I wanted to ask you — you got any further use for that stage station property on the Cibolo? I want to buy it. On credit. For El Bar headquarters."

Fitzpatrick chuckled. "No more use now than a hog's got for Sunday. Heard about you. Take the blamed place, pay what you can, when you can."

Dewey said, "Thanks, Fitzpatrick. That settles that. Now —"

Doc Orr said, "He's got to shut up and lay down."

Carlos said, "I want to hear what went on last night in Trevino's house. Up to the time our crowd hit the place."

Dewey told it, including the news that Navarro had delivered May Gibbons across the river to Sorro. "I'm damn glad to have some help on finding her, Carlos."

"I'm sorry." Carlos shook his head. "We can't cross the river. Tonight we've got to make our big try for Navarro and Tembler. We have the best chance now we ever had to grab them with the stolen Sorro horses. It's enough to give us a case — to fill this jail with 'em till we can move them all into Austin for state charges and trial. But I'm afraid we can't help you any on the girl, much as I hate to say it —"

Dewey struggled to his feet. "Then, by

God, I'm going over there."

Doc Orr firmly pressed him down to the cot. "You ain't going anywhere."

A man hurried in at the jail office door, cradling a Winchester. "Good news, I think. The men posted west say nobody's ridden from town toward the west crossing since daylight. Chances look good that word of last night hasn't gotten to Navarro yet. If we can keep the town ringed off till dark, we still have surprise on our side when we hit the herd force."

Carlos said, "By the way, Lane, I took the liberty of reading a message the stage agent got, addressed to you from Austin. The inquiry you sent about Rusty Ferris. Dan Blocker of the Austin newspaper investigated. The extradition order Navarro claimed to have for one Rusty Ferris was a forgery. Thought you'd like to know. By the way, who *is* Rusty, Lane?"

Dewey felt angered, somehow. Disappointed, frustrated, at outs with all of them. "That's my damn business," he muttered. "You don't want to cross the Rio, then by God you run your business and I'll run mine."

Peyton Evans coughed. "Reckon he told you, Ed. Now, any of you boys besides me of a mind to take a little jaunt to the Sorro fandango with him?"

Dewey heard Carlos's firm reply. "I'd like to, you can be damned sure of that. I'd like to include Sorro in this haul. But it can't be done. South side of the Rio Grande is one place where we can't go, girl or no girl."

Doc Orr, sometime back, had shot a needle into Dewey's arm. The tiny pain prick of it remained. The big pain in his tightly bandaged side floated away in a haze, but the pinprick of the needle remained as a far-off red star, hanging crookedly, a freckled star mocking him with song.

17

There had been a great amount of muffled going and coming from the jail all afternoon. Dewey sleepily listened. After a long time he roused to full wakefulness, sat on the edge of the cot, then tested his strength by standing. The bandage around his middle held tautly, the pain had subsided. There was no sun now, only a pinkish glow at the barred window. The sounds and the voices had ceased.

Walking to the doorway, buckling on his gun, he saw a young man with a shotgun on guard in the hallway. The guard grinned and asked, "You feeling better?"

"Fine. What's become of everybody?"

"They're headed for the west crossing. The big crackdown's due out there tonight. Carlos said if you started meanderin' around to tell you to get back in bed."

"Yeah. How far is it out there?"

"Ten miles. But you're not to go."

"Did I say I was?"

"Look, Carlos said to keep you here. I can't tie you down or shoot you. I just told you what Carlos said."

"You did your duty. Where'd they leave my horse?"

"At the back, in the corral. I wish you'd stay put."

"I might ride a way west, just for fresh air. *Adios*. Keep your eye on the high sheriff."

He walked out into the dusk, saddled the black in the pen, and was pleased to find that his Winchester remained with his saddle gear. As he rode around the jail building, he saw a rider coming in a hurry from the business district. The outline in the saddle looked familiar, and Dewey pulled up, squinting hard at the oncoming figure of Rusty Ferris. They met a short distance out from the jail.

"Told you not to come."

"I get town fever occasionally."

"Your fever's worse than that, considering the wound in your shoulder."

"From what I learned just now in town, you're not much better off. Good thing I had the itch to come in and see about you. Pa and the rest stayed at the stage station."

"Damn it, Rusty, where I'm going is no place for a sick man —"

"Who's got reason to want Sorro in his

gunsight more than me? C'mon, let's catch up with the posse. Heard all about the deal from Ponch, at the Lady. He's been a tipoff man for the Citizens Committee."

Dewey shook his head. "You won't find Sorro out there. He's holding a celebration across the river — they've got May over there. After the showdown tonight at the crossing, I'm asking some of the citizens bunch to cross over with me, to help me bring her back."

Rusty's jaw hardened. "Navarro did that? He sent her to Sorro? Then let's be riding. I know the crossing."

Dewey shook his head doubtfully. "Two cripples. Between us we'd nearly make a whole man. Let's go."

They left the town in the gloom behind them, walking their horses side-by-side along the west road above the river. Dusk turned into night and the faint course of the trail dimmed. Brush, gullies, and rocky ridges blended into one vast layer of shadows. After an hour, Rusty said, "We're getting close now. Keep your ears open."

Two horsemen emerged from the darkness ahead, rifles swinging.

"Hold up there! Who is it?"

They identified themselves to the lookouts.

One of the men said, "Last I saw of you, Lane, was in the jail bed. But I guess we need all the guns we can get. The horse herd was on this side, in the flat, about a mile up from the river. Startin' halfway out, we got men scattered in the roughs, two teamed up together, and everybody's job made clear. They start moving in at straight-up ten o'clock, which time's not long off. They expect to find the Tembler outfit driving the horses north. Two hundred Mexican mustangs ain't going to be hard to locate. Their riders will be strung out, some on the flanks of the herd, some at the point, most on the drag. Horses are damned mean to drive. We've got near fifty men. We hit from all sides, two going for each Tembler rider. I reckon you might as well pick you a team to join up with, and get to work."

They asked a few more questions, then started to ride on. One of the road guards said, "First of our men you run into may be skittish, dark as it is. You better take it cautious and use our password. it's 'Governor Coke.'"

Dewey and Rusty rode on. The silence and darkness under a low overcast of clouds seemed to Dewey to become a live and evil thing, closing in on them. Somewhere near, now, in this blind night, fifty men waited to liberate a town and regain their own rights. Most of them ordinary business men, citizens, clerks, merchants of Laredo, all sizes and ages. Doing a job because Texas had paid them scant notice, had sent no Rangers because of the Indian trouble in the Pecos country. All at once Dewey had his strong doubts. It was an awfully black night; the vigilantes, for all their courage, were up against some tough professionals. They might take some of the outlaws. But how were they going to be sure they had two experts like Navarro and Tembler in their trap when nobody could see man or horse a rod ahead of him?

Some of the wrong men were going to be killed tonight, he thought. Some of the prisoners they wanted were going to get away. And if anybody did, it would be Navarro.

As he turned this over in his mind, Rusty slanted his horse closer and whispered, "Somebody just ahead, there. Watch it."

Dewey made out the denser shadows in the low cedars. A voice called quietly, "What's the word, you two?"

Slowing, Dewey called back, " 'Governor Coke.' "

"You got an assignment?"

"No. We got out late —"

"Not time, now. We're movin' in. See that

knoll yonder? They're passin' just to the east of it, about a quarter out from the bottom. In the flat. Listen and you can hear the herd movin'."

Dewey caught the faint churning of many hoofs. He eased his horse back a little. The two riders ahead now cut northwest from the trail, toward the black outline of the knoll. Rusty, with an eager word to Dewey, kicked his horse to a trot, catching up with the other two. Dewey let him ride on alone. He waited until all three had gained a distance that put them out of sight.

His hunch might be wrong. But he had to follow it. If it proved wrong, if he missed the fight, his absence wouldn't make much difference, one way or another. If they thought he had dodged the dirty part of it, let them think it. But if Navarro gave them the slip, he thought, the chances were about ten to one that the deputy would put all his craftiness and scheming into saving his own neck. That meant to Dewey that Navarro would strike for the river crossing, try for escape to Mexico.

He headed toward the river. Once he came across a pair of riders who swiftly cut his trail, murmured the password on their challenge, and kept to his own course while they vanished in the darkness on theirs.

When the sounds of the north-walking horse herd drifted past, and to his right, he circled southward a little more, to be certain he avoided any far-back drag riders. He rode among stunted trees on ground sloping sharply toward the river. As he cleared the growth and emerged in an eroded open space, a thin light came on to etch the scene in grayish illumination.

The moon. Not much of a slice of one, but a little, breaking through patches of the overcast. The land took on a ghostly visibility. A high, startled yell swelled up from the gray distance and bounced itself along the arroyos. Ten o'clock. A gun shot, the wild forerunner of a pack of shots that followed, cut the yell down at its high-pitched zenith. In the next moment Dewey heard the night break apart with battle. He guessed Rusty was in the thick of it, maybe wondering if Dewey had got cold feet.

Still, he kept his downgrade course, contending with the black's nervousness and his own, holding his rifle ready, listening to the eruption of gun fire northward. Plainly, the Sorro mustangs had stampeded in the first commotion of the attack. He could hear their flying hoofbeats rattling the earth, almost drowning out the shooting. He came to the edge of the open shelf sloping to the shallow river now visible on his left. The tracks in the earth, the chopped-up turf told him this was the crossing.

He needed to get to the better cover on the west side of the open ground, and sent the black across in a running spurt. On the other side he worked into a shadowed gully, blending his mount with the rock out-croppings. He could only hope the commit-tee's plan had worked, that the Laredo forces were taking prisoners. For a moment he felt like a deserter, a soldier who had holed-up to avoid the battle. He put the guilty feeling out of his mind because a rider was headed his way, circling toward him through the brush at his back.

His horse moved, tossing its head, and he tried to quiet the black. The rider neared, but with odd fits of starts and stops. Who-ever he was, he was watching things, taking his time and not rushing into anything. Not coming down the open grade that entered the crossing either, but from the northwest angle through the brush and roughs. Dewey brought his rifle up.

The man halted just inside the screening bushes as if studying the open space. Then he emerged and rode toward Dewey and the river's edge beyond. He kept close to the pro-tecting brush, holding his horse to a walk, turning his head swiftly to watch all sides.

He was a big man, and that was all that Dewey could make out. Dewey raised his rifle, and the oncoming horse began tossing its head.

Softly, holding the figure to his gun now, Dewey called, "Password, mister."

The rider made a noticeable jump and slapped his hand to his holster gun. " 'Governor Coke.' "

So he was probably a lookout, sent to watch the crossing. Dewey relaxed. "All right . . . How'd it go back there?" As he said this, Dewey coaxed the black out of the brush. He lowered his rifle, trying to make out the man who now had turned his horse a little, making himself sidewise to Dewey.

And as Dewey emerged fully into the thin moonlight, the other, too, cleared the shadows and they stood revealed to one another. Belatedly, the voice tugged warningly at Dewey's memory. Now he felt bludgeoned, no muscles and no voice at all.

Navarro laughed harshly and fired. The shot raked Dewey fiery hot across his shoulder blades and spun him out of the saddle. He landed on his hands and knees, with the black cutting up between him and Navarro, and then rolled himself tumbling into the shadows, trying to draw his Colt.

Navarro's gun smashed fire at him again, the slug shattering weeds at his face. Dewey felt something give at his rib bandage, and collapsed to all-fours once more. Navarro fired once again, and the bullet knocked Dewey's leg out from under him. He could not get up in time, for Navarro was swinging off his horse now and advancing with leveled revolver.

"I'll stomp the livin' damned . . ." Navarro's words faded to a crazy mumble.

He thinks I'm done for. Dewey lay motionless in the shadows, and watched the deputy stalk toward him. Then, when Navarro stood over him, raising high his booted right foot, Dewey tightened his clenching hands, all his fingers, like squeezing a sponge, on the Colt braced to his stomach. The gun went off almost in Navarro's face, the snout of it poking straight up, the slug taking Navarro in the mouth. Dewey saw the blood gush out, darkening Navarro's whole lower face. Navarro tried to lift his gun, but he tottered, fell heavily and started beating the dirt weakly with his fists.

Dewey felt the assault of pain. When horsemen came crashing out of the brush at the upper end of the crossing, he called to them, and hoped that Doc Orr might be among them.

There were four, but no Doc Orr. They turned Navarro's body over, then two of them started methodically to work on Dewey's wounds. Another man came from the north, running his horse. Dewey heard Rusty's voice. "Is that Lane? What happened to him?"

The man doing the bandaging replied, "He's not so bad hurt, no bullet inside, just slug gashes, leg and shoulder."

"Anyhow," said one, "he sure as hell stopped Navarro when it looked like he'd given us the slip. How did he get so close to Lane, I wonder?"

Dewey told them. "He said the password. He was trying to make the river, and he knew the password."

"Somebody squealed, then," a man said. "Or else he overheard some of our crowd using it. This was a pretty confused business when we first hit. Anyhow, Navarro caught on and dodged the trap."

"Well, he was about the only one," another commented. "And he didn't get far, thanks to Lane."

"Jake Tembler is in handcuffs, Frank Hanson is dead, all the rest under guard except four of their bunch who took bullets and maybe as many more that slipped through," Rusty reported. "We lost three men. I'd like to have taken this one myself. You outguessed him, Dewey."

"That other business," Dewey said quickly. "Sorro. May Gibbons — You men willing to ride with me to find her?"

"We've gone as far south as we can, Lane," the spokesman said. "I'm sorry. We've got all the work here we can handle. Now two of you help Lane, get him on a horse and up to Doc Orr, where the fire is. You others, let's get back to those prisoners."

Dewey found himself cursing as the group rode out of sight. Two men remained. One of them was Rusty.

"You gave me the slip." Rusty went over and looked at Navarro's body. "So did he."

"He spoke the password. Got right on me. Rusty — how far back to Nuevo Laredo from this crossing?"

"Too damn far."

"I'm going."

Rusty looked down at Navarro again. "So he spoke the password?" He added flatly, "I know how he got it."

Dewey and the other rider stared hard at him, waiting. Finally Rusty said, "He high-tailed for the brush when we hit and he was about the first one I recognized. I wasn't far behind him, because I was watching for him, trying for a shot. One man headed in and Navarro threw a shot at him, and this one got rattled, I guess. He yelled, 'Governor Coke, damn it!' thinking Navarro was one of our bunch. Navarro caught on *Pronto*."

"Who was he?" Dewey demanded.

"We'll never know. Navarro shot him dead. I saw him fall and Navarro took off. I lost him in the melee. We've got three hands dead — who'll ever know which it was that spilled the beans? But that's how Navarro got that 'Coke' business — he worked his way right back through our rear guard with it."

Dewey pulled himself into his saddle. He said to the rider who had remained to help him, "Suppose you head on back to the crowd at the fire up there. Rusty, you stay."

"Where you two goin'?" the rider demanded.

"Tell Carlos — you just tell him that I've gone to a fandango."

The man started to argue "He said for you —"

Dewey said curtly, "Ride on! Leave Navarro's body here for a while, send a horse for him later. Right now I need his clothes. Mine are ripped and bloody."

18

Dawn touched the taller Madre foothills and this was about as near the Mexican settlement as they could safely get. Two slow wraiths, stumbling and hurting, they holed up in the brush at a canyon water pool like clawed coyotes. After short-staking their horses in grass, they stretched dead asleep as soon as blanket rolls were spread.

In the afternoon they roused and crippled to the horses, watered at the canyon hole, and downed cold rations from Rusty's saddlebag. Then Dewey set about the final business, for it was time for him to ride.

He unrolled the bundle of clothes. He put on the jacket and pants he had taken off Navarro because his own were bullet-ripped and too bloody to wear anywhere. He refastened to the jacket the weighty silver law badge that Navarro so arrogantly had worn. He tossed the handcuffs to Rusty who had been reloading the three Colts with clean rounds.

Rusty grimaced. "Just the sight of those things make me sick."

"Don't accidentally get yourself locked in 'em while I'm gone. I didn't find the key."

"Don't worry, Deputy! The big thing is for you to convince Sorro that you can trade me for May. You just bait him to come get me, then Big Mex will find out mighty fast how I can get out of this damned jewelry."

They exchanged a final look. All had been said that there was to say. Dewey lifted his hand. "*Hasta lueguito.* Stay put and stay ready." He turned the black to the east.

First the settlement came into sight, a darkened straggle of sod-log houses, then the rank smells, and the yapping of the peons' dog packs. He felt the villagers' eyes boring him from the dark doorways, and the Texas side of the river seemed half the world away. He tied at the Casino's rail on the plaza among rifle-hung mustangs. After taking a quick look back, he roughly pushed the scarred doors and entered with the heavy-footed assurance that he thought a Laredo deputy might have shown.

The Casino proved to be partly a high-walled open courtyard, with roofed-over bar on one side and second-floor gallery rooms showing at the far end among a riot of vines and deep shadows. He walked on the packed clay floor to the bar at his left, conscious of his and Navarro's holstered Colts on his legs, the silver law badge showing in the sputtering lights, and his nagging wounds. Sombreros turned at bar and tables, a dozen or more heads following him. The outlaws' shoulder bandoliers rattled with their movements. He stood at the bar, taking them in impassively. The men he saw were heavily armed, coarse in their features from years in the weather or from old fighting scars; the girls, hard and scarred from their own form of banditry.

A yellow-shirted stubby man, with Colt and knife in his wide belt, turned his bull shoulders, thrust his companions aside with a heavy hand, and advanced, frowning at Dewey's badge. He brought a bottle by its neck.

"For the moment," he said in English, "I took you for Blackie Navarro. But they say Navarro is dead, the others in the calaboose. You escaped?"

"So you have heard about our losses?"

"*Sí.* Is it bad over there?"

"Very bad. I came to inform Sorro."

"He will want to hear. And you, Deputy — you are a new man to me. Do we know you from before?"

"Navarro hired me as a deputy after Lenman got killed."

"But you escaped last night. That is good."

"About the only one who did. They hit us hard."

The Mexican extended his bottle. "I am Victore, the lieutenant of Sorro. You have heard of me?"

"Navarro told me that you were Sorro's strong right arm." *So did Rusty!*

"No, I am strong *here!*" Victore grimaced and touched his gun butt.

Dewey said, "Permit me the honor of buying the next bottle. . . . You must have had quite a fiesta last night. Mescal flowing, I guess. Girls, music, singers . . ."

"Ah, *mucho gayo!* Until the bad news came from across the river. Tomorrow we move south."

"Sorro's still around, is he?"

Victore lifted a thumb toward the gallery rooms at the rear. "Up there."

Dewey asked casually, "The girl singer — she will perform tonight?"

"The Texas *cantora?* Of course. Then Sorro will take her with us to the mountains. She is his new favorite." He winked broadly. "Let us sit and drink, amigo. We have music, girls, good times. . . . If you cannot return to your town because of the trouble, you may wish to travel with us."

More outlaws and a sprinkling of town men in ragged clothes drifted in from the night. The vino and mescal aromas laced the other odors of old body dirt, smoking oil lamps, saddle sweat. The musicians at the rear went to work with guitars and fiddles, and the girls came, mingling with the noisy throngs at bars and tables. Two of them attached themselves to Dewey and Victore. The Sorro lieutenant at once chose the chunky girl with the heavy breasts, and thereafter worked his vino bottle with one hand.

The slender girl with the thin scar along her cheek said, "My name is Carmelita." She sat on Dewey's knee and encircled his neck with bare brown arms. "Big gringo law man!" Her fingers toyed with the law badge. "You are new to us. And Carmelita found you first. You have money, *si?*"

"Later. I'm waiting to see Sorro."

She swayed and grimaced. "Sorro has a new girl. The Texas singer. But you have Carmelita. Navarro got himself keeled. Now I will be your girl."

Victore grunted, "Here comes Sorro's singer."

Dewey almost spilled Carmelita from his

lap, craning to see. She clutched at him, but he managed to sight the small figure of May Gibbons where she had stopped at the far end of the courtyard in front of the four musicians. He saw her primly smooth her flaring Spanish skirt and begin her song. Talk and quarreling quieted. Victore muttered, "Sorro will soon tame that proud little *cantora!*"

May's profile turned. Dewey stiffened, waiting. Then their eyes met.

The light was poor. Smoke floated between them. But her glance found him after stumbling past once, and he knew the moment of her startled recognition. The song faltered a beat as her voice gave way, caught up again, and her head jerked haughtily when Carmelita intimately touched the wine bottle to Dewey's mouth. Dewey shoved her aside. Victore and his girl left the table and vanished after May's song was finished.

The noise and milling resumed, and Dewey lost sight of May. He removed Carmelita from his lap and deposited her in a chair. Wincing against the pull of his wounds, he pushed back from the table, muttered, "We need more vino!" and left her looking hurt and murderous. He pretended to head for the bar, moved among the drinkers, drifted toward the rear. Light touched his law badge, dark eyes shifted beneath low hat brims. He went unmolested. For a time, at least, he was accepted as Navarro's man, Victore's good friend.

He found himself in a darkened walkway among a maze of crannies and partitions beneath the second-floor portion of the adobe walls. He called softly, "May!" hoping that she had waited for him. Her answer came from a near-by tangle of vines that smothered the outlines of a massive stone column.

"*Dewey! Dewey Lane!* Over here!"

In another moment he was finding her hands, feeling the excitement in their warm grasp.

"You are foolish to come here."

"Quickly now! Are they watching you? Can we get away — ?"

"No. No! It would be foolish to try! Guards everywhere. I would be seen —"

"I want to know now — did he — has he harmed you?"

"No. The news of trouble across the river stopped everything last night. It is tomorrow that I have feared, when they leave here, starting for Sorro's place in the mountains."

A shadow fell across the wall. A heavy hand tore into Dewey's shoulder, whirling him about. He saw the towering giant, heard the muttered words and May's gasp: *"Sorro!"* He stopped his own gun hand short of his Colt. The massive figure caught May's arm, pulling her forcibly into an embrace. "My little singer forgets who pays her. She must not be so free with her affections."

May's struggling carried them across the walkway into the faint light at the balcony steps. As Dewey followed, an eruption of high-pitched Spanish words bore down with a frenzy of feminine anger. Carmelita hurled herself upon him and he had to fight off the clawlike attack of her fingernails. It was Victore, close behind her, who grabbed her bare shoulder and jerked her about. Laughing, Victore said, "Control your jealousy, my fine *puta!* Or you will find your beautiful body hanging by the thumbs."

May, who had been released by Sorro, staggered Dewey with an unexpected temper flare of her own that almost matched Carmelita's. "Take her back to your table and your lap! One girl to the evening should be enough for you, *señor!*"

"Easy, now!" Dewey muttered, realizing what May was doing.

Sorro and Victore seemed to think the scene very funny. Carmelita struggled out of

Victore's grasp, her blouse ripping open, and then she came to a freeze before a flashing steel blade leveled in the smaller girl's steady hand. May said fiercely, "Come at me with those claws and I will take the pelt of a wildcat!"

Dewey, intently watching the massive, mustached Sorro, saw the humor drain out of the bandit leader's lumpy features. Sorro's scowl worked on him. He mumbled to Victore, "This is the man you told me about?"

Dewey answered for himself. "Navarro's deputy. I escaped the trouble last night — and I have important business with you. My time is very short. We need a place to talk —"

Sorro looked him over again and made an abrupt motion to the stairs. "I want all the news I can get. Bring the deputy up here, Victore."

Victore swept the sulky Carmelita aside. Dewey said, "The girl, too — this singer. She has a part in the business to be transacted."

Sorro paused, "The singer is my business only, Deputy."

"I think you will be interested in what I have to say. There is more for you than this singer."

Sorro shrugged. "Victore told me that you were the only one who escaped. I will hear what the new deputy has come to report." He turned and trudged up the stairway. Dewey nodded to May, seeing the uncertainty and inner fright, and they fell in behind the bandit leader, trailed by Victore.

In Sorro's room, the big man stalked about nervously. "Tell me your business."

May Gibbons stood aside, watching, listening, a small and lonely figure. Dewey could give her only one, quick, significant glance.

"I escaped the trap at the crossing because Navarro had sent me on another job. I am glad to tell you that I was successful. We lost our herd that you delivered, we lost everything, as you have learned. But in this one job, I did not lose. I have succeeded in finding and capturing a man you badly wanted. More than that, I have slipped him across the river, to this side, against great odds, and I can take you to him."

The stare of the bandit held. Sorro let his cigar droop wetly from his mustached mouth and cocked a brushy eyebrow. "This prisoner — would he be the one who escaped from Navarro?"

Dewey nodded. "The same."

Sorro massaged his massive hands. He

mumbled two words, low and throaty. *"Rusty Ferris."*

May gasped. Her hand went to her mouth. Dewey watched Sorro, seeing May only from the corner of his eye. "The same. I am here to talk trade."

Sorro thrust his thumbs in his belt. He laughed shortly.

"The new deputy should know that I am the one who decides. In a trade with Sorro, there are never any terms but my own. But I will hear you. What you have said intrigues me very much."

"What is he worth to you?"

"A good price, I can tell you. Where is he?"

"Safely in custody, at a place where he can be delivered to you before you start south. Now, do you wish to know my price?"

Sorro shrugged and grinned wolfishly. "Why not?" Humorously, he spoke across to Victore at the door, "We have a bold one here, Lieutenant."

Dewey looked directly at May. "I will trade Rusty Ferris for this girl. Sorro will understand — Ferris was not an easy one to take alive, and I have my own reasons for wanting the girl." He showed a brief grin in response to Sorro's short chuckle. "Sorro has many girls. But there is only one Rusty Ferris."

The bandit chief scowled. "It would be worth much to me to stand him before a firing squad." He added viciously, "He killed my son. If you can lead me to him, you may take the girl for your pay."

"I have something to say about this!" May glared at Dewey. "I'd rather sing for the bandits the rest of my life than —"

"You are excited, *señorita*," Dewey said quickly. Was she acting, or dead serious? "Rusty is nothing to you, nor to me —"

"This is treacherous!" May said angrily.

"Trouble already in your ranks, Deputy." Sorro squinted at one, then the other. "This one, she is a prairie fire! I had meant to tame her when time permitted."

"Like a contrary horse I once had." Dewey nodded. He looked hard at her. "Name was Cibolo. Very *tricky!*"

He saw May's expression change, and quickly shifted his attention to Sorro. "Time is important. I left my prisoner handcuffed to a tree in a canyon not far to the west. I would like now for you to go to the place with me, and the girl with us, to complete the transaction."

Sorro deliberated. "Very well. Victore, get horses. A dozen men. Sober, if we have that many."

257

"No." Dewey set his jaw. He had Sorro well on the hook. "No men for this, *señor.* Just you and the girl."

"And why?" Sorro stiffened in suspicion.

"I would trust you to go through with the trade, as a man of your word. I know you want custody of Ferris. Your men — I would not trust drunken men at night with this girl —"

"My men follow my orders!"

Dewey was groping for an answer when May alertly furnished support.

"I will have the say, I think." In movements like an assured, stretching cat, May came forward languidly, in a twisting movement, touching her braids. "I say only Sorro. I have no taste for this, nor for a *crowd* to see me traded like — like a mare for a goat! Yes, that is how it will be. Otherwise, the deputy can keep his Rusty Ferris and I will keep to my singing in the Casino. After all, this is small matter to me."

Dewey disguised his admiration. Sorro grinned broadly. Dewey, as if she had humiliated him before the others, roughly caught her arm, jerking her to him. "You'll do what *I* say — you damned, fickle —" He secretly pressed her arm. He saw her stiffen and tear away violently.

"I can stay with the great Sorro and be

paid much silver," she said indignantly. "I do not have to submit to —"

"Shut up!" Sorro boomed. But he laughed with enjoyment. "Deputy, what you would want with the freckled imp, I cannot see. *Dios!* Let us ride. Victore, four men, I think. Enough. *Vaya pronto!*"

May's glance to Dewey said that she had done the best she could, and it was really better than Dewey had hoped for. Might have been a dozen, instead of four. Sorro, he believed, had no suspicions yet, though it was impossible to read him with certainty. When they were all assembled in the street, Dewey led the riders into the night, sided by Victore, with Sorro and May riding next, and four rifle-slung outlaws trailing. He speculated that the surly guards might have been instructed to give him a volley in the back, as soon as the trade was made. Sorro no doubt intended to ride back with Rusty *and* May.

The light of the moon bathed the canyon edge. Dewey held up his hand, looked back as the others bunched up, said, "Over here."

Sorro got down and peered blinkingly into the shadows. Beside him, Dewey said, "Yonder tree. Don't worry — he's hand-cuffed and helpless." Victore levered a cartridge. Sorro muttered, "Lead the way, Deputy."

They advanced, and the moonlight revealed the man's form prone at the base of a sapling. Rusty sat up, awkwardly gaining his feet. The pale cast of light touched handcuffs, for all to see, where they held his left wrist, apparently locked to the tree. May had worked her horse near them.

Dewey took off Rusty's hat, revealing the hangdog cringing of the prisoner, slapped Rusty across the face with it, roughly crushed it back upon his head, and faced Sorro. "Well, here he is. All yours. The girl and I will ride away now. Step up and claim your prize." He made a small motion, seeing that May intently watched him. She edged her horse to one side, and all eyes held fastened to Rusty. Dewey pretended to fish for the key. "Sorro may come forward and have the honor of unlocking him."

Sorro squinted a long time, and then said with heavy relish, "The one all right!" He squared his great shoulders, exhaled noisily, and stalked forward. "It will be a pleasure."

Rusty appeared to sink his chin into his chest at Sorro's approach. Sorro slapped Rusty in the face, twice, forward and back, with the palm of his hand.

May Gibbons moaned, and Dewey said,

"*Now, Rusty* —" and made his move, fast, but making sure he did it right, with no bobble, drawing his Colt and smashing it accurately across Victore's temple, knocking the lieutenant senseless to the dirt.

In the same eruption of motion, Rusty flipped his left hand and it came free of the manacle. At the same time he reached behind him with his other hand. It came around with his sixgun that had been concealed in his belt at the small of his back. Dewey spun Sorro about with a gun slap to his ear, and then both of the gringo Colts were pressed hard to the bandit's spine.

"You know what'll happen if —" said Dewey.

But Sorro already knew, and halted the bunched play of rifles with a command to his men, "Don't shoot me, you fools!"

Dewey said, "*Tell them to ride!*"

Sorro called dazedly, "A trap! *Vamoose!* Get help! They will kill —"

After confused hesitation, the four men turned their horses and rode away. Dewey and Rusty lost no time. In a matter of seconds, they were riding through the brush, toward the Rio Grande, herding Sorro ahead and watching out for May who had no chance to say anything in the rush. When they came out on the river bank, Rusty called, "This is no good. Bad current along here."

Dewey stared down at the whirling depths below the embankment. "We can't go back to Nuevo Laredo to ford, and the horse crossing is a long way west."

Sorro stayed glumly silent, eying the dark flow of the river with evident fear. "*Señor*," he finally muttered, "I cannot swim."

May said quietly to Dewey, "I never knew you would look so good to me, Dewey Lane. Even with the Casino girl on your lap. It's been so fast tonight — a dream, still. I'd try swimming it here, anywhere. Just to get home."

"You did your part," he said gruffly. "You've got brains —"

She said thinly, "You think that's all?"

"Damn it!" Rusty exclaimed. "Listen behind us — hear that?" He jerked on the lariat extending from his saddle to the tight noose about Sorro's waist. "What did you do, Big Mex? Have your whole damned army trail you?"

"Sounds like it." Dewey listened. "Plenty of horses coming."

Rusty said, "If I know this big *bastardo* like I think, he gave orders for his outfit to follow him. He's always leery of a trap. Those four guards didn't have to ride far to get reinforcements." In an undertone, he added, "I wanted to deliver him alive in Texas, but I doubt if we can do it now, and I haven't got the guts to kill him in cold blood."

"Free the rope and crowd him in the water ahead of us! Hurry, now! May, try to swim your horse close to me," Dewey said.

The horses balked at the steep descent, and Sorro protested in a wild flow of Spanish. Rusty freed him of the rope. They worked down to the rocky shelf and into the current. Rusty used his lariat to whip Sorro's horse ahead of him. The sky had darkened with the spread of a cloudy overcast, and the water seemed to turn black where it yawned to the opposite unseen bank. Back of them, quite near, they heard horses breaking through the brush, and a high yell.

Now the four horses had lost footing and were swimming, bunched at first, with Rusty crowding Sorro ahead, Dewey trying to slow his to allow May to keep up. The black was swimming strongly and pulling ahead of May's horse in spite of Dewey's efforts. The undertow in midstream asserted a noticeable tug, starting them all on a drifting curve down river. Faintly, above the churn of the horses, sounds broke out on the bank behind them. A rifle sent the first splash to the surface in their midst, and then a whole barrage of rifles winked in flame, and bullets spattered everywhere. Thankfully, Dewey knew they had passed from clear vision, were swallowed by distance and cloudy darkness. The firing ceased. They would be afraid of killing Sorro. The night behind swallowed the last evidence of pursuit. Dewey looked for May, who was almost out of sight.

She called calmly, "My horse is floundering, I'm afraid —"

Dewey tried to pull his horse toward her voice. He had almost reached her when, to his left and ahead, Rusty shouted, "Hold on there, dammit!" Then, "Dewey! Where are you? Sorro's disappeared off his horse!"

Dewey had his own hands full. He struggled to force the black against the current's pull until May's horse was near. Then he lowered his right leg from his balance atop his saddle, kicked out viciously and caught the other horse a raking slash in the rump with a spur. May hung to her saddle, submerged to her waist, as her horse responded. It took on new effort with the spurring, churning wildly, and then the flailing hoofs struck bottom.

The horses clambered out, blowing,

struggled to the rock slope, and Dewey groggily dismounted and helped May down. Every move he made came with pain from his reopened wounds. He stretched weakly to the gravel. He was losing blood. Rusty loomed ghostlike to his drowsy vision.

"The river got him," Rusty said as he and May sank to the river bank beside Dewey.

Dewey murmured, "We tried to keep him alive. We did our best."

Rusty sighed. "The Rio Grande served him all these years. And then it cut him down. I kept hearing him holler, that water was washing him out of sight, and then no sound at all, no sign, no Sorro, just the current. . . ."

It was midnight and a week later when May came into the room adjoining her own at the Laredo Lady. Dewey was still up and dressed, still weak in the legs, tightly bandaged where Doc Orr had sewed the gashes in his shoulder and leg. May had waited on him in the daytime, and had performed as a solo singer at night on the Lady's stage. Evans, Carlos and other townsmen had been in and out to visit him. The days were foggy to his memory, but he felt his strength returning now, bringing a sudden, revived interest in things, and a worried, disgruntled feeling about May Gibbons that he couldn't quite define.

She stood in the doorway of his room, which had once been Cherry's. She had just finished her act and still wore her low-cut, bespangled stage dress, and her face was dabbed with makeup. She eyed him sharply, then came in frowning.

"Why aren't you in bed?"

"Why do you want to keep performing for that mob of wolves downstairs?"

"Because, in case you didn't know, I get ten dollars a night for it from Maceto, and *somebody* has got to pay the bills for —"

"Well, that's over." He glared at her getup. "Wash that stuff off your face. Get into some other clothes —"

She stared back, at first angrily, then calculatingly. "Yes, *sir*, Mister Lane!" She meekly withdrew, closed the door, and he paced the narrow confines of the room. A week, was it? He had to get back to El Bar. Rusty and Joe Barton had been in, and said they were established in the old stage station now, with Hagerman and Benecke helping, everything ready for Dewey to start building his ranch. He ought to be out there — regardless of what Doc Orr said about lost blood and wound infection. A hundred things to be done. He turned as May opened the connecting door.

She stood there in a plain gingham dress, the stage makeup removed and her nose freckles shining through the scrubbed little-girl look.

She said coldly, "This suit you better?"

"Yeah. You look decent now."

"All right. Now that I'm dressed to please you, what do we do?"

"We get out of this damned whore house —"

"*Mister* Lane!"

"And cut out the damned *mister*. Pack your bags."

"Midnight's no time to start somewhere."

"All right, we'll leave tomorrow — but pack anyway."

May murmured in a stage voice, "Listen to the man give orders."

He walked toward her. "I believe you actually like to sing in a place like this — stage struck, that's what you are. Never would be contented on a cattle ranch. No, you've got to have footlights and a drunk mob of men taking you in, and —"

She tossed her head defiantly. He reached for her with his arms. She moved quickly and his reach fell short. Her hand went down, her skirt came up to her thigh, and a shining steel blade flashed out of her garter. He stared at the knife.

"This stopped Sorro, and a few others. You've been burning with something beside bullet fever ever since I've known you, ever since you first saw Cherry. Well, don't think you can start all over with me."

Very carefully, he took her chin in his hand. He lifted her head and forced her to look at him. Suddenly, she twisted her head away, and he pulled her close with slow relentless pressure, and the knife hand limply went down, relaxed, and the blade dropped to their feet. He kissed her. "Tomorrow, we go home."

The next morning, when he was already dressed and packed, May knocked at his door and timidly entered.

"The buggy will be here soon," she told him. "Mr. Carlos said we might return his horse any time that's convenient."

"Did you tell Maceto you were quitting this job?"

"Yes. I drew my pay. Do we need to take out supplies? Altogether, I have nearly two hundred dollars, after paying —"

"I've got some credit." He grinned. "Just save it. Time will come when —"

"Ponch will carry down the luggage. I guess we start — home — soon."

The Cibolo crossing was tame, this time, and Dewey had no trouble bringing Carlos's rig down the slope from Laredo Road at dusk, into the rocky trickle, and up the other side.

"There it is," Dewey said. "Our new El Bar headquarters."

Peering excitedly at everything, May suddenly called, *"Cherry!"* Then they were in the station yard. May and Cherry embraced. Dewey stiffly climbed out, favoring his stitches, and the house and grounds began erupting people who came on with a babble of greetings. Ma Barton greeted May first, then Dewey. Rusty and Joe stalked about, and Hagerman and Benecke stood by, grinning, until it was their turn to shake hands.

Mrs. Barton said, "You're just in time for supper."

Dewey smiled at her. "Figured so. This is sort of where we all came in, isn't it?"

In a little while they moved to the long table and hesitated. Dewey seeing this, sensing the slight awkwardness in Hagerman, in Benecke, and all the others, spoke across to Hagerman. "Don't suppose any of that whisky was left?"

Hagerman moved agilely, and Benecke helped him pass the whisky cups to the men. Mrs. Barton said, "Just one, now. Supper's getting cold."

"Now, Ma —" But Joe Barton's words were cut off by her firm expression.

Dewey said, "Joe, if you will sit at the head, please — and Ma, at the foot. Rest of you, anywhere."

He sat beside May, with Hagerman next, and Cherry, Rusty and Benecke across the table. Everyone had his say, bringing the others up to date, but refraining from more than bare reference to the bad times. Later, when the coffee cups were refilled, Benecke cleared his throat. "I'd like to hear Cherry and May sing again. Just like it was that night — over there by the door where you were, Rusty."

Cherry said, "Come on, May."

"I've quit singing."

Turning, Dewey saw the mischievous twist of her mouth corners, then the pink tinge surfacing to her cheeks.

"I think it would be all right, here," he said gravely.

"Well, if you think so . . ."

She joined Cherry near the door to the small room. Cherry complained, "We'll miss the Lady's piano player," and May said thinly, "Oh, I don't think so."

They sang as they did before, except that the strain and nervousness were gone.

"*Mañana* must be, say *sí* . . . say *sí* . . .
See the sun stealing near, Chula
    Chalita . . .
Whisper in the night, tonight, this
    night . . .
Dream of this night *mañana,* my Chula
    Chalita. . . ."

With the words of the song, May's attention played flittingly upon Dewey. He twisted his legs nervously under the table. Then, at the last *mañana,* as if the puzzlement showed all over him, a dance of small, appreciative lights came unrestrained into her eyes, and with them a decisive smile, her detached look gone and a woman kind of certainty showing impudently in its place.

He smiled back at her, in case she didn't already know his mind, which he doubted.

Rusty spoke knowingly across the table, "When this family handcuffs a man, Dewey, he never gets them off!"

Dewey looked up and down his El Bar table, to May returning sedately to her place beside him. To Rusty, he said, "Who would want to?"

We hope you have enjoyed this Large Print book. Other Thorndike Press or Chivers Press Large Print books are available at your library or directly from the publishers.

For more information about current and upcoming titles, please call or write, without obligation, to:

Thorndike Press
P.O. Box 159
Thorndike, Maine 04986 USA
Tel. (800) 257-5157

OR

Chivers Press Limited
Windsor Bridge Road
Bath BA2 3AX
England
Tel. (0225) 335336

All our Large Print titles are designed for easy reading, and all our books are made to last.